Five Children

Layla Prichett

Contents

The First Meeting

Annabel hummed a cheerful tune as she walked uphill, opposite of the large streams direction on her left.

The cascading sun rays made the water shimmer and glisten. The fish darting inside were as visible as the mansion in the far distance. Their scales were a bright silver, and you could even see their gills expand with each breath they took.

As she continued to walk upstream, a continuous little squeak caught her attention.

"Oh my."

She rushed to the water's edge and sat on her knees.

"How did you end up here you poor little thing?"

A wet, shivering, baby squirrel sat digging it's little claws into the rock he was on, trying to hold onto dear life and not get swept away by the current.

"Don't be scared now. I'm going to rescue you."

She slipped off her slip on shoes and bunched up her slightly longer than knee length dress as she stepped into the freezing water.

The squirrel was luckily on one of the few shallow parts of the very large stream, and Annabel was able to reach him in no time.

"It's a good thing you aren't that far away from shore. I can't swim." She smiled down at the squirrel who was edging its way closer to her and holding a paw out. "I got you."

She slowly reached her hand down as to not spook him on accident, and he hurriedly climbed on.

"Here you are. I'll keep you warm. How did you get down here? Where's your mummy?" She slowly made her way back to the shore and slipped on her shoes with one hand, and tried to warm him up by holding him close to her.

The side of the stream she was walking on was the clear, grass field side, with a dirt road not far away, not a single tree was in sight other than the cluster of three trees closer to the far away mansion. There's no way the squirrel had come from there. The only possible explanation was that he was from the forest on the other side. He must have fallen into the water from his nest and somehow, in his panic, swam all the way over to the side she was on.

"Don't you worry. I'll take care of you until you're strong and healthy. Then you have to look after yourself and go back to your friends." She wrapped her thumb around his little body, giving him extra warmth and picked up her bag with her free hand and continued to the mansion.

"You're late." The butler said when he opened the door upon her arrival. He was nearly an entire head taller than her. His eyes were a piercing brown, cold, calculating. His tailcoat went all the way down to his knees. The bow tie sitting just below his chin was more put together than her life ever was and his hair was white and fluffy as snow, although he had it combed and gelled back.

The foyer was one of the most impressive she's ever seen. A large chandelier hung up, rugs rolled out on the polished floors, stairs that led to the top floor, part of its hallway looking down on the foyer. Straight in front, past the round table right under the chandelier were large double doors leading to what seemed to be an extraordinarily large dinning room with a long dinning table. The right seemed to be leading to a living room and to the left were the stairs. Under the stairs was a large closed door that she couldn't tell where it led to.

"I'm terribly sorry, I was just-"

"It does not matter. Master Richard is expecting you in his study. Follow me."

"James! Don't be so mean to her. She's only just got here." A petite round women slapped the butler with a towel and pushed him away so she was standing in front of Annabel.

"Hello dear. I'm Samantha, the cook! Don't mind James, he might seem cold but he's actually really sweet and kind. He cares a whole lot about Master Richard and his kids." Samantha's brown, greying hair was up in a bun with strands coming out of it. An apron was wrapped around her waist and it had blotches of sauce and flour. Her hazel eyes and round figure were inviting and looked very motherly with her plump cheeks and yellow dress.

"I'm Annabel, it's so lovely to meet you." The woman offered her hand to Samantha, but she pulled her into a hug.

"The older kids are with their father in the office, while the twins and the baby are in the play room, drawing. They shouldn't bother you while you're getting-" James, the butler, began to say before he got interrupted.

"Hello."

They all turned their heads to the ground where two five year olds were holding hands with a three year old.

"Hi." Annabel put her luggage down and crouched so she was up to their height.

"I'm Sam, this is my twin Tam and this is our younger sister Margot." He held out his hand looking all professional with his dress pants, waistcoat and tie.

"I'm Annabel." She shook his hand and offered him a smile that he did not return.

"Are you our new nanny?" Tam asked.

"I believe so."

"Then we do not like you." Sam said and Tam nodded. Margot saw Tam nodding and copied her.

"That's alright, everyone's entitled to their own opinions."

They looked her up and down before turning around and leaving.

Annabel watched with amusement as the door under the stairs opened for them, two sets of eyes stared at her before ushering the children in and shutting the door.

*

"Well, how did she do?" Maggie, the second oldest of the Pelton siblings, and only 15, asked the two five year olds.

"She said everyone's en, en," Tam tried saying the word but had a hard time.

"Entitled Tam, it's entitled." Sam said and walked over to his father who was sitting in his fancy armchair behind his desk.

"Enwitelted to their own obenions." Tam proudly said and Margot clapped for her.

"I reckon that's a positive start." Richard Pelton picked up his son and placed him on his lap.

"Indeed it is. The other nannies would get really upset and scold them." George, the oldest Pelton sibling, at 17, spoke up from his seat on the couch.

"Yes, but she did arrive 10 minutes late." Maggie crossed her arms and rolled her eyes. She did not want a nanny.

"10 minutes is not the end of the world." Her father said.

"It's unprofessional for a first meeting." She shot back and normally, Richard will tell her to watch her tone, but he knew how much each time a new nanny came, her stress will be through the roof, so he let it slide.

A knock on the door told them that James has brought Annabel, so the kids all sat on the couch, from oldest to youngest, and they all sat up straight watching the door like hawks, even Margot.

"You may come in, James." Richard spoke up and the butler held the door open for Annabel and when she stepped in, he closed the door and stepped out.

"I'm glad you could make it." Richard got up from his chair and walked over to her, arm extended. He couldn't help but notice just how pretty she was with her soft facial features, loose braided brown hair and slim body. He wasn't used to seeing anyone other than Maggie with their hair down. Everyone else always put it up or cut it short.

"Thank you. Although I am really sorry for being late." She placed her hand in his and he lifted it up to his lips and pressed a gentle kiss against her fingers.

She blushed and pulled her hand away.

"Yes, ten minutes to be exact." Maggie grumbled from her seat and George nudged her.

Annabel gave her an apologetic smile when she felt something move in her pocket. Everyone's eyes trailed down to the moving pocket.

"What's in there?" Sam asked.

Margot hoped down from her seat and made her way to Annabel, she closely watched the pocket and tried poking it.

"You have to be gentle." Annabel said and sat down on her knees. "Or he'll get really scared."

"Scared?" Margot asked and Annabel nodded.

Sam and Tam ran over to see what she was pulling out of her pocket.

"This is why I was late. It was a life or death situation, I had to save him." She opened her eyes wide and exaggerated her facial movements which got the kids even more excited.

"Well go on, what is it?" Even Maggie and George made their way over in the little huddle. Richard peered from on top as she slowly began pulling out a baby squirrel in the palm of her hand.

"A baby squewel!" Margot clapped her hands and the squirrel ran up Annabel's hand in fright and stood at the crook of her neck.

"He's just a baby, so he's still very sensitive to noise."

"What did you name him?" Maggie went back to her seat.

"I haven't thought of a name yet. Would you like to give him one?"

"I can?"

"Of course."

"How about Squeak?"

"Very original Maggie." George rolled his eyes and plopped down beside her.

"I think it suits him well, don't you?" She looked up at Annabel who nodded at her. "See, she thinks so."

"I hope it's okay with you." She looked up at Richard and stood back up on her feet. "He won't stay long, just until he's big enough to take care of himself."

"Of course, now let's discuss what exactly it is you will be doing here and the room you will be given."

Settling In & a Prank & a Challenge

Annabel felt like she was constantly being tested by the children in the week she has stayed with them so far. Whether it was them testing her nerves and being difficult on purpose, causing a large mess, or testing her on their school material for some reason. She was going to prove to them that she wasn't a horrible person like they thought she was and she was actually there to help, she wasn't the enemy.

No matter what the children did to Annabel, they felt like they couldn't get her to quit, pack up and leave. And the longer they spent time with her, the more they didn't want to actually have her leave. She was fun, kind and very understanding. She treated them fairly and age appropriately, never making them feel like they were inferior and she respected their thoughts and opinions. More importantly, unlike the other nannies, she didn't flirt with their father and try to do indecent things with him just for his money. They kept things professional, although friendly, but still professional.

"How are you settling in dearie?" Samantha knocked on the slightly ajar bedroom door and stepped in.

Annabel was given a fairly large room on the second floor, not one in the maids section of the house. This way, she could get to the children, if they needed her, faster. Her room consisted of a nice little living room, with couches and a heater for winter and the room also included a small book shelf for the few books she brought with her. The living room opened up to the bedroom that had a vanity, a closet, and door that led to her own separate bathroom.

"Just dandy, I think the kids are finally understanding that I'm not a horrible witch like they originally thought I was." She said from her comfortable seat on the couch, book in hand.

"And why do you think they thought you were a witch?" Samantha laughed and sat down on the one seat couch.

"I had tucked the little ones into bed and started cleaning up the mess they had created in their playroom adjoined to it, when I heard Maggie sneak in to them. They were talking in hushed voices about Annabel the witch. It was actually very comical. I might dress up as a witch one day just to give them a scare."

"Serves them right those little rascals. They've really been up your hair, more than anyone else."

"It's quiet alright really. They're all lovely deep down. I see the way they interact with each other and their father. A lovely little family they are." Annabel sat up right and glanced towards the open door, Samantha doing the same. "I hope I'm not overstepping when I ask, but do you mind telling me what happened to their mother?"

Samantha bunched up her apron nervously and quickly glanced at the door.

"Listen well dearie, I love to gossip, I do, but this is not for me to say. When they feel comfortable enough, the kids, they will tell you." Samantha heaved a sigh and got up. "Well, I have to get going. It is pretty late. Sleep well."

"You too. Would you mind closing the door on your way out, please?"

"Of course."

*

Annabel woke up the next morning feeling very refreshed. She sat up and swung her legs to the side and slid off the bed. She held in a shriek and gasped really loudly when her feet landed in cold, gooey, wetness.

A shiver ran up her spin in shock and she curled her toes and slowly looked down to find she had stepped into a pan full of chocolate fudge and whipped cream.

She took a deep breath through her nose and calmed down, a smirk making its way onto her face.

"Oh you've asked for it now you naughty little rascals."

Throughout the day, random screams were heard coming from the four eldest children.

Annabel had set traps for each and everyone single one of them with the help of Margot, and got them all covered in whip cream one way or another.

"Father!" Maggie screamed and marched to her fathers office. She barged in, only to find three of her other siblings already in there; and they all looked like her, covered from head to toe with whip cream.

"I see you're covered in whip cream as well." Richard tried his hardest to hide his amused smirk.

"You find this amusing!? You can't let her get away with doing this to us. Fire her immediately!" Maggie stomped her foot and crossed her hands.

"Now now Gigi, don't you think you might be overreacting slightly? Who are you even talking about?"

"That blasted Ms.Annabel, who else? If you-"

"Watch your language young lady. That's street talk and I will have none of that in my house."

"Yes sir, but you really must do something papa." She grumbled.

"I think she played fair." George spoke up. "You three did prank her in the morning. Which got me in this mess. I'm more upset with you guys." He sighed and got up.

"I'll go to clean myself up, excuse me." He nodded to his father and left the office.

Outside, he passed Annabel with Margot and when they passed each other, they high fived.

"You got her good." He said heading up the stairs.

"Now she won't pull that nasty prank again." She called back as she and Margot went to the kitchen to find a snack.

*

"I challenge you to a race." Maggie barged into Annabel's room.

"I would prefer it if you knock. Could you please knock first." Annabel said from sweeping her floor.

"Do you accept?"

"What's that? I think I hear something." Annabel pretended to look around the room for something by looking in every direction but Maggie's.

Maggie groaned out loud, stomped out of the room, shut the door and knocked.

"May I come in?"

"Ah! It was Maggie I was hearing. Of course you can come in. Can I help you?" She put the broom aside and gave the girl her full attention.

"I challenge you to a running race, today, an hour after lunch. If you're not there then I take that as your defeat, and my win."

"Well, I never back down from an honest challenge."

The two shook hands.

By the time the race was scheduled to start, everyone in the mansion had heard of it and they were all coming to watch. The horse handlers, maids, James, Samantha, the kids and even Richard.

"I hope you're ready to lose." Maggie looked her up and down when they took their positions at the start line.

"You do realize my legs are longer than yours?"

"I thought you don't discriminate."

"I was just pointing it out."

Phil, one of the horse handlers raised a hand to signal that they should get ready.

Both of them slightly lifted their dresses and took off when Phil put his hand down.

Annabel knew Maggie wanted this to be as honest as possible so she didn't slow down or let the girl win just to make her feel better. She pushed her legs forward and smiled at the feeling of the wind blowing in her hair that had fallen out of the thin black ribbon holding it in place.

Richard had originally come down to cheer his daughter on, but when he saw Annabel he couldn't think of anything or anyone else. He was focused on the smile on her face, the wind blowing in her hair, the look of pure happiness as she ran across the field and crossed the finish line first. He walked out on the field and picked up her the hair ribbon that had fallen out of her hair and stuffed it in his pocket.

All cheering came to a stop when Maggie tripped and fell hard, only a few yards short of the finish line. Annabel quickly rushed over and pulled the girl onto her lap.

"Maggie? Maggie are you alright?"

When the girl didn't respond, Annabel peered into her face and noticed the tears falling and the shoulders that began to tremble.

"Did you get hurt Gigi?"

"Get away from me!" Maggie pushed her away and pulled her knees up, wrapping her arms around them.

"I just want-"

"Why do you care!? You're not my mother! Stop caring! You're just lying! All of you horrible, evil nannies do. All you want is papas money. I don't want you here. I want my mama!" She hurriedly got up and ran back inside the house.

Annabel sat there in shock as she tried to process what this little girl had said.

She didn't blame her for her outburst. It was natural, expected. To her, Annabel must be looking like someone that was replacing her mother and wanting to take advantage of her father. Maggie didn't trust her because that's what everyone else has been trying to do.

A single tear of sympathy for the girl rolled down her cheek before she quickly brushed it off.

Sympathy isn't what Maggie needed right now, she needed someone to be there with her.

She began to get up and someone helped her by placing their hand on her elbow and pulling her up.

"Is everything alright? Is Maggie okay? Are you hurt?" Richard searched her face.

"We're alright, thank you. But I really need to go talk to Maggie, she needs someone right now."

"I could go if it would-"

Annabel shook her head no.

"It's quite alright Mr.Pelton, I need to talk to her. Don't worry yourself." She gave him one last smile and went into the house to look for Maggie.

She gently opened her bedroom door to find the girl softly crying into her pillow, still in her dirt and grass stained dress.

"Go away. I don't want to talk." Her muffled voice spoke up.

"We don't have to talk if you don't want to."

Maggie sat up and wiped her tears away when she heard Annabel. She wasn't expecting her to be the one to talk to her after what she's said. She expected her father to come tell her off for being rude.

"What are you doing here?"

"I noticed your knees were slightly bleeding." Annabel held the first aid kit up and walked over to the girl. She sat on her knees in front of a sniffling Maggie and began cleaning her cuts and wrapping it up.

She heavily sighed when she was done and began packing to leave.

"I'm sorry." Maggie wiped her nose with her sleeve and looked down to her lap in shame. "I shouldn't have screamed at you like that."

"It's alright. I understand."

"But you wouldn't."

"My father and brother both passed away in the same year, I think I understand a little bit."

Maggie looked up in surprise and saw a few tears well up in Annabel's eyes at the recollection of her brother and father before she brushed them away.

"Was it...was it..." Maggie couldn't even finish asking the question.

"It's still hard. I just got better at dealing with the pain. Look Maggie, I never meant to make you feel like I was taking over your mothers spot. I'm not. And I can't. No one can. A mothers place is special in their children's heart and no one can fill it up once they're gone. I'm also not trying to steal your father or his money. I'm here for you, for George, Sam, Tam, and Margot. I'm here to help in the best way I can. I'm really sorry if at times it might have seemed like I overstepped my boundaries or pushed your buttons. Truce?"

Maggie nodded and flung herself onto Annabel as she began to full on cry at finally having someone understand her pain.

"It's okay, you can let it all out." Annabel wrapped her arms around the fifteen year old and held her tight.

*

All five kids, Richard, and Annabel were in the spacious study room. Richard had a desk for himself that he was sitting in, doing his paper work. A round table was in front of him occupied with school work and books. A few couches lined the length of the room and a fireplace made the room all that more cozy. Although it didn't get used that often.

"In previous centuries Western Europe lived under feudalism and mano- rialism. The people identified with the manor they lived in or with Chris- tendom rather than with King or country. It's because the King had little to no influence over anybody, but that changed when manors decided to unit into kingdoms and people grew a sense of-what was it called again?" Maggie recited out loud to herself while she walked back and forth along the room.

"Nationalism." Annabel spoke up from helping the twins with their simple math problems.

"Yes, that, thank you."

Annabel and Richard shared a look and he had a happy smile on his face. That was the first time Maggie said thank you to her.

"Right, and that fostered kings and queens because of the sense of loyalty people had for their own states." She continued to speak while Annabel ruffled Sams hair at getting the question correct.

"So what do you think Tam? If I had an apple, and you had an apple, how many would you have if I gave you mine."

"Two!" She said and held three fingers up.

"Excellent. Except two is actually like this." She put one of the fingers down on her hand but it popped right back up.

"Doubt thou the stars are fire; Doubt that the...that the moon?" George groaned and fell into a chair.

"Doubt that the sun doth move; Doubt truth to be a liar; But never doubt I love..." Annabel continued the lines from Hamlet for him and he continued on when he remembered it.

Richard looked up from his paper work to his hard working family and Annabel. They were all moving along in their studies and seemed to be enjoying themselves. They had to grow and mature so fast with their mother's passing and with the constant flow of nannies coming in and out of their lives. They seemed to finally be letting things loose and be children. Actual children that played in the yard, teased, laughed, ran in the house, and just be happy. He noticed George was slightly backing off on helping with raising the kids and was attending to his studies again. He had always wanted to be an architect, but those dreams stopped when he had to help look after the kids. Maggie wasn't being so uptight anymore and her true kind self was resurfacing, something he was sure had to do with her and Annabel's talk a few days ago, and the twins were getting along and starting their schooling. Margot was more of a happy baby and she loved just hanging around Annabel. He'd often find the two together immersed in some sort of crazy activity or out on a stroll around the house. He was very thankful for Annabel, she was helping bring his family back together and he hoped that she would be sticking around for a while.

The Injured Leg

Another week passed and Richard was soon called back to the army to attend to his duties there as a general.

"I'll look after everyone, don't worry." George patted his shoulder and for a fleeting second, Richard saw a grown up man ready to take on the world.

"I'm sure you will." He ruffled his eldest sons hair and moved on to the second oldest.

"You better come home safe or I'm not ever going to forgive you." Margot kissed his cheek and he pulled her into a hug.

"Not even if I bring you chocolate?"

"I'll consider it."

He kissed the top of her head and then crouched down to the twins.

"You better not give Ms.Annabel any trouble while I'm gone."

"Of course not!" Sam saluted and Tam followed. He kissed both of their cheeks and stood back up to meet with Margot who was being held up by Annabel.

She handed him his daughter and stepped back so they could have their moment.

He hugged her tight to his body and kissed her head several times.

"I don't know how long I'll be gone, so you better not grow up too fast." He kissed her cheek and she laughed and held onto his cheeks and smoshed them together. He smiled and handed her back. The last time they called him back, it was for half a year to help settle some things after the Second World War. He really didn't want to be gone for that long.

He stood expectantly in front of Annabel and raised a brow when she looked at him with confusion.

"What? Are you not going to say goodbye to your boss?"

"Goodbyes are forever." She looked him in the eyes and tried to focus on them, and not how good he looked in his uniform.

"Then I'll see you later." He was about to lean in but stopped himself once he realised what he was going to do.

"I'll see you. Come back in one piece though."

"I'll try."

*

George and Maggie talked in hushed voices together in the library and immediately stopped when they noticed their nanny and younger siblings walk in.

"What's all the secrecy for?" Annabel teased and walked to the young kids section to read them a book. The twins took off to find one.

"We'll see you at dinner." Maggie got up, pulled her brother with her and rushed out of the library.

"What do you think those two are planning?" She asked Margot who was trying her hardest to climb onto a chair.

"Party." She said and managed to pull herself up, but was stuck with facing the splat of the chair. Annabel picked her up and turned her around.

"You think? They'd plan a party as soon as their papa isn't home? I don't think so."

The twins ran back to her with the book they had chosen and she began to read to them until it was time for dinner.

*

"We need to talk to you." Maggie said as soon as Annabel stepped out of the kids room after tucking them in for bed after dinner.

She looked between the two siblings and their serious, stoic expressions.

They sat in their fathers office. They had Annabel sit on the couch and them on the two one seaters facing her.

"This all seems pretty serious."

"It is." George said and Maggie nodded.

"Don't tell anyone, but we think papa tried to kiss you today, on the lips." Maggie said with the most serious face.

She looked between the two of them, suddenly all the hushed whispers made sense and she burst out laughing.

"That's what got you so consumed all day?" She continued to laugh. "I'm sorry, I shouldn't be laughing. This isn't funny is it?"

She looked at their faces and burst out laughing again.

"I'm sorry, I really am. But where in the world did you get that absurd idea?"

"So he didn't?" Maggie asked.

"I told you he didn't! You were just seeing things!" George exclaimed and slouched in the chair.

"But I could swear he was about to lean in. I saw him!" She jumped up and glared at him.

"Don't you think Ms.Annabel would know if papa tried kissing her?"

They both turned to look at her.

"Don't worry, he didn't." She assured them and for some reason it seemed like they were slightly dejected.

"I see, good night then." Maggie dragged her feet along and pulled George with her. They went back into hushed talking and Annabel couldn't be more confused.

*

A month has nearly passed since Richard has left and although the children missed him terribly, they did get weekly letters that made them feel better.

They had also grown closer to Annabel and began to regard her as one of them. They really enjoyed having her around. She was fun and spontaneous. Always thinking up activities and things for them to try. They would go on picnics, play the American game called baseball with the horse handlers, have arts and crafts activities, play in the mud, ride horses (although she didn't know how to, so it was their mission to teach her), stay up past their bedtime at times, mess with the butler and bake with Samantha. They even released Squeak back into the wild and he would come and visit them every now and then.

"Ms. Annabel, a letter addressed to you." James held out a letter to her when she walked past in the foyer and she thanked him with a confused look. This was the first time she receives a letter.

She went into the kitchen, found a seat and opened the letter. She read the contents of the letter and worry and anxiety grew inside of her.

It was a letter from Richard, but it didn't hold any happy news.

She immediately told Samantha and the two of them told the maids so they could get his room ready and anything else they needed.

"Why does everyone seem to be moving around more?" George asked her when she hurried past him.

"I got a letter from your papa."

His eyes light up and he fell into step with her.

"Is he coming home? Is that why everyone is scrambling?"

"Your siblings are all in the playroom, yes?"

He saw the grim expression on her face and knew whatever the letter held, it wasn't good.

"I need you all to listen up please." She said and everyone turned to look at her when she walked into the playroom. Margot ran over to her and asked to be picked up, but George was the one to do it.

"What's that letter in your hands?" Maggie pointed out the letter.

"It's from papa." She said and took a seat on the ground with all of them, George following .

"What did he say?" Tam put a hand out asking for the letter and Annabel handed it to her, even though she couldn't read.

"Well, to put it shortly, he's coming home. Today."

Maggie cheered in happiness. Sam and Tam hugged each other and jumped around. George smiled from ear to to ear and Margot clapped but she didn't know why.

"But, but not because he's done with his work."

"What does that mean?" Maggie grabbed a piece of her dress as she looked at Annabel's worried expression.

"Once someone is called in, they are only allowed to temporarily leave for a funeral or leave because," George's eyes widened in realisation at what she was saying. "Because they're injured and can't continue to serve either temporarily, or forever."

"No, papa can't be hurt."

"His right leg. He can't even move it and because of that, they're sending him home and he's retiring." Annabel said.

"Papas hurt?" Tam asked and tears rolled down her cheeks while Sam tried to wipe them away.

"It's okay Tam. Papa is strong." He told her and kissed her cheeks.

"Exactly. Which is why when he arrives, you all will not be sulking and ruining his already bad day. Be happy he's at least back and that he's alive. Now, go get ready, he should be here soon." Annabel picked up Margot to get her changed and took Tams hand who took Sams hand.

*

"Welcome home papa!" The kids ran to their father once he entered the house in his wheelchair pushed by the nurse behind him. They hugged him as best they could with the wheelchair and propped up leg being in the way.

"It's good to have you back." Annabel walked up to him and gently placed Margot down on his lap when he held his arms out for her.

"It's good to be back." He smiled up at her, but then winced in pain when Sam accidentally brushed his injured leg.

"Papa is really tired and hurt. Why don't we head to the playing room and give him time to rest?" She took the younger kids, promising them that they will go back later to see him again, and walked to the playroom.

"Welcome home sir." James greeted and motioned for the horse handlers to help carry Richard and the wheel chair up the stairs and into his room. "Master Richard, I hope you are hungry." He said.

"Famished." He winced again as his leg jostled back and forth.

"Be careful, you're hurting him." Maggie said and hurried up the stairs and to his room to get the door open.

"How has everybody been?" Richard asked once he was placed in his bed, his leg was adjusted into a more comfortable position, he was sitting up with pillows all around him and there was no one else other than him, George and Maggie.

"Ms.Annabel has been wonderful with us and the young ones." George said.

"Yes, there's never been a boring day with her. She can do many amazing things." Maggie said.

"Yes, but get this, she can't ride horses."

"And you've been teaching her?" Richard asked.

"Of course we have! She can even trot around the ring now."

"Papa don't you think Ms.Annabel is just so beautiful?" Maggie stretched her arms out to the side to show him how beautiful she was.

"Ah, I mean, umm, where is this coming from?" Richard was caught off guard with the question. "I was asking about you guys, not Ms.Annabel."

"Yes but she can cook and read and sing and write poetry, she can even ride a bike, and makes the most amazing sandwiches for our picnics. She's very creative and fun and also very kind and loving. She's a wonderful person papa." Maggie stared into his eyes and he shifted in his seat.

"I'm sure she is, that's why I hired her. Now, tell me about you."

"Well, Ms.Annabel -"

"No not her, you." Richard said to George.

"Are they not letting you rest?"

They all turned to the door where Annabel was standing and it was as if Richard was a deer caught in headlights. He did greet her earlier, but he could only get a good look at her now, and it seems she somehow got even prettier than the last time he saw her.

"I told you she's beautiful." Maggie whispered in his ear and bounded out of the room, not before giving Annabel a hug on the way out.

"I'll leave you two be. I still haven't finished my studies for the day." George got up and on his way out he kissed her cheek.

"They seem to have grown to like you even more." Richard said as she walked in and sat on one of the two pulled chairs beside his bed.

"It does seem so. They're all very wonderful children."

They lapsed into a few seconds of silence when her eyes fell on his leg.

"How bad does it hurt?"

Richard looked at his leg from studying her face and sighed.

"A lot. And I wish it was at least from doing something heroic but it's not." He sniggered at himself.

"What happened?"

His breathing slightly hitched and he swallowed hard when he realised that she was also studying his face.

Annabel blinked and looked down at her hands

"Just a freak accident with training some new recruits. It's hard to tell when I'll be able to walk again on it. Maybe never."

"I know it might be hard, but try to be a bit more optimistic about it. At least you're here and still alive."

"I'll try."

They lapsed into more comfortable silence again and it was Richard that broke it this time.

"Ms.Annabel, you have a, an eyelash on your cheek."

She flushed with embarrassment and tried to brush it off.

"No it's more," he motioned to a spot on his cheek and she tried again, "no no, it's closer to you, here, let me do it."

He gently placed his hand on her extremely soft cheek and glided the pad of his thumb under her eye, brushing the eye lash off.

His eyes fell down to her pink lips and he subconsciously began to slowly lean in.

Her eyes opened wide and she quickly pulled away from him, cheeks flushed, ears burning.

"I'm sorry. That was very unprofess-"

"Thank you for brushing it off. I'll get going and leave you to rest. You must be very tired." She hurriedly got up and walked out of the room. She shut the door and leaned on it, placing a hand over her fast beating heart, trying to settle herself before she went to find the nurse and tell her that he wanted to rest and might need help with laying down.

Richard groaned out loud when she left and threw his head back at the head rest at his stupidity.

"You're a respectable man Richard. Pull yourself together." He scolded himself.

But what was he supposed to do when his heart beat speeds up around her? When he finds himself following her movements with his eyes when she's in the same room as him? When he loves it that his children love her and she loves them? That he loves how smart and simple she is? And that without even trying, she's the most beautiful thing he's ever seen?

How was he supposed to not grab her, kiss her and tell her how much she drives him insane but that she also helps keep him sane?

How could he not do that?

Mama!

Annabel took the twins and Margot out to the field so they could play. She promised Tam that she would teach her how to make a flower crown out of the dandelions that grew everywhere.

"Yes, and you put it through, yes! Just like that, that looks wonderful Tam!" She kissed the top of the girls head who's smile stretched even further.

"It's for you!" Tam got up and placed the sloppy crown on Annabel's head.

"Thank you, that's very kind of you. Would you like the one I'm making?"

"Yes please!"

Sam ran over to them with a finger held out.

"Look at what I found Mama!"

"What did you fi-wait what?"

"Look at it! It's so tiny." He held his finger out for her to see. She glanced at the ladybug on his finger and smiled up at him.

"A ladybug, I haven't seen one in a while. Sami, can you please have a seat?"

He sat down crisscrossed and looked up at her with his big brown eyes. Annabel quickly glanced up at Margot to check on her and was glad she was playing in the grass only a few yards away.

"Look Sami," she scooched closer to him and took his hands in hers, taking careful notice to not spook the ladybug. "I know I've been taking care of all of you for nearly four months now, and that's a long time isn't it?"

He nodded.

"And I love you very very much, you need to know that, but Sami my love, I'm not," she took a deep breath. "I'm not your mama. I'm just Annabel"

"I know."

"So why-"

"She's gone. Died because she was really sick, but I don't really 'member her. You love me, and I love you like my mama. Tami and I love you like our mama. Right Tam Tam?"

Tam nodded.

Margot ran to them on her chubby three year old feet and held out a daisy she found to Tam, but changed her mind and gave it to Annabel.

"You're not mean like the other nannies, you're really nice and fun. And I don't want you to leave. So please be my mama." Sam got up and put the ladybug on the dandelion crown on her head.

"I - I don't, look, I can be, but you can't call me that. It's unfair to your papa, mama and Maggie."

"Okay."

"Mama? Where?" Margot asked.

"She's up there." Annabel pointed to the sky and they all sat on their backs and watched the rolling clouds.

The children soon fell asleep on the grass and Annabel didn't have the heart to wake them up.

"I never knew clouds could be so entertaining."

A shadow fell on her and she turned her head back to see Richard.

Standing up.

She sat up and half turned around to look at him.

"You're standing!"

"With the help of this cane, but yes." He smiled wide at seeing her smile and fill with excitement for him.

"Did you walk here all by yourself?" She was so incredibly happy for him.

"James helped me down the stairs."

"I'm so happy for you. But the doctor said it was okay to start walking around?"

"Yes."

Sam stirred in his sleep and they quieted down.

He limped over so he was beside her and sat down. They both laid down on their backs and looked up at the sky.

He slightly turned his head to look at her peaceful relaxed face. Her eyes were closed and she was drinking in the sun light.

He glanced down at her hand and made a move to grab it but stopped himself. He shouldn't.

"Don't you find it very therapeutic Mr. Pelton?" She turned her head and looked at him. Their eyes meet and her heart skipped a beat.

"What?" He softly said and noticed how her skin glowed in the sunlight and how it made her cheeks a slight rosy pink.

"Relaxing in the sun."

"I think it makes me sleepy."

"I think they would agree." She looked at the children and a smile adorned her face. She really did love them.

"Look at them, looking into each other's eyes like there's no one else in the world." James grumbled from the window. He let go of the curtain and turned away.

"I think they look very adorable. What if Master Richard and Annabel fall in love? Do you think they would make cute babies?" Samantha let out a dreamy sigh and followed James into the kitchen.

"That will not happen. She works for him and Master will no way fall in love with her crazy behaviour."

"Love works in mysterious ways my dear James." Samantha kissed his cheek and patted his chest.

"Yes yes I know." He pulled her back to him in a hug and she giggled.

Carnival Games

"Come on let's go!" Maggie called out from the front door.

Her siblings rushed down the stairs. George was carrying Margot and the twins ran past him and out the door.

They were all ready and dressed hours before they were supposed to leave for the carnival that their papa promised to take them to. The carnival was going to stay in town for only three days and one day has already passed.

"Papa walk faster! You're being very slow!" Sam had the window rolled down and his head was poked out the side of the car, calling for his father that was making his way slowly over to them with that ever prominent limp and cane in hand.

He laughed at all their excitement and made his way to the passenger side.

"Is everybody ready to go?" He looked back at them, their faces were all lit up.

"We're waiting on Ms.Annabel." George said.

"Mama said she's not coming." Sam spoke up.

Everyone turned to look at him and Richard drew in a sharp breath.

"She's not mama." Maggie said, glaring at him.

"Call her Ms.Annabel." George shifted Margot on his lap and rested his head on the window, feeling uncomfortable.

Richard cleared his throat and shifted in his seat.

"Why isn't she coming?" He asked and ignored the look the driver was giving him. He could't yet drive with his leg still being bad.

"Really? That's all you have to say? You're not even going to correct him?" Maggie's cheeks grew red in anger. "Our mama is dead. There is no other mama."

She climbed over the twins, opened the door and rushed back into the house shouting over her shoulders for them to go on without her.

"We'll wait. She'll calm down and come back." Richard leaned his head back and sighed. "You kids can go play on the grass until she gets back."

"Hey, I was just about to rush out and hand you guys this basket of sweets Samantha made." Annabel said when she saw Maggie rushing in.

"You're a liar!" Maggie screamed at her and ran up the stairs with tears running down her face.

A hurt expression made its way on Annabel's face and she looked out through the open front door of the house to see what was happening.

Her and Richard held eye contact for a few seconds before she hurried after Maggie.

"Gigi?" She softly knocked on her bedroom door and opened it, immediately ducking at a pillow being hurled at her head. "I understand you're upset about something, but that wasn't very nice."

She picked up the pillow and went over to the couch the girl was sitting on.

"What have I done to make you feel like I'm a liar?"

She didn't answer her.

"I won't know what I've done wrong if you don't tell me."

She still didn't answer her.

"Look, I'm sorry for whatever you think it is I lied about, but I probably didn't. I'm not one to lie and you know that."

"But you would lie about wanting to replace our mother."

"And why would I do that?"

"So you could get father to fall in love with you and steal his money. You don't even love us and you never really cared about us!" Maggie turned her body away from Annabel and sniffled. She wasn't about to lie to herself and say that she didn't wish Annabel was different than the other governesses that came to look after them, because she did. She hated having people look after them without actually wanting to. Although, she knows she's overreacting.

"That's hurtful of you to say Maggie and ridiculous of you to think." She pulled the girl closer to her and wrapped her arms around her. "I'll repeat it as many times as you need hearing. I'm not here to replace your mother. I never was and never will. No one can, really. And of course I care and love all of you. If I really didn't, do you think I would have tolerated everything you did at the beginning? Don't you think I even would have began to treat you horribly in your father's absence when he wasn't here to over see everything?"

Maggie stayed quiet and rested her head on Annabel's chest. Loving the feeling of having her hand run through her hair in a calming manner.

"Sam called you mama." She whispered what was really bothering her.

"He did that didn't he?" Annabel kissed the top of Maggie's head and pulled back to look at her.

"Sam and Tam lost their mother in a very very critical time for their development. I'm not saying you didn't, but they really needed her to be there for them. I'm not sure if you realised this, but they had to grow up so fast and do things all by themselves a lot faster than they should have for their age. They and Margot crave that motherly feeling more than anyone else, and the second someone shows them a little kindness, love and appreciation, they will most likely get attached to that person and start seeing them as a parental figure."

"But Samantha is also kind to them, so are the maids, why didn't he ever call them mama?"

"It's different. They're not looking after them all day long like I am, now are they? They have chores to do, their main job. Helping the children comes second to that. My main job is to look after them and help them learn and grow, it's only natural that they start feeling like this."

Maggie cuddled closer into Annabel and put her head back on her chest.

"Are they forgetting mama?" Her voice sounded horrified at the idea.

"Margot more than the twins, but I would guess so."

"I'm scared."

"Why's that?" Annabel began combing through Maggie's hair again with her fingers.

"Because I'm forgetting mama."

"Why don't you write down what you remember?"

"I-I can't remember almost anything."

Annabel held the girl closer as she began to cry again.

"Well, I've never met or seen your mama before, but I can kind of tell what she looks like."

"You can?" Maggie sniffled and looked up at her.

"She had blond hair, didn't she? Just like George and Margot. You and the twins have brown hair like your papa. And her eyes were brown like yours, Sam and Margot. And Samantha, she said that you have your mothers ears." She playfully tugged at Maggie's ear and the girl giggled. "Tam has your mamas nose and I hear she was about this tall."

She lifted her hand up and Maggie nodded.

"I also know more, but first, you need to wash your face. We don't want your siblings waiting too long now do we?"

"What more do you know about mama?" Maggie asked after she was done washing her face and fixing her hair as they walked down the stairs hand in hand.

"Well, I assume she's the one that played the piano because none of you have touched it since I got here. And your papa sits on the left side of the table during tea time, so she must have sat on the right. She loved horses, that's what Phil, the horse handler said. Her horse is still in the barn, her names Biscuit, but she's a very old mare and her back is too sensitive for any riding or harnesses. You could go and brush her if you'd like. See, your mama is everywhere. You just have to look and you will remember."

"Thank you. You're the best ever!" Maggie hugged her tight when they were standing outside and ran to her family who were waiting for her on the grass.

Annabel smiled at them greeting Maggie happily and turned around to go back in.

"Ms.Annabel!"

She turned back around to look at Richard.

"Won't you join us?" He asked.

"I think I'll pass Mr.Pelton." She waved at the kids good bye, glanced at a defeated looking Richard one last time and headed back in.

*

"How are you feeling Gigi?" Richard walked through the carnival with his daughter while George took the younger ones on the carousel.

"I'm okay. Feeling a lot better after crying and talking with Ms.Annabel."

"That's good to hear."

"Yeah, she helped me remember what mama looked like, I was forgetting."

"Forgetting?" It pained him to hear that one of his children was forgetting what their mother looked like, but that was expected. Even he was having a hard time remembering what his late wife's voice sounded like. "I have a picture of mama, would you like to see it?"

She stopped in her tracks and nodded in excitement as he pulled out his wallet and the black and white picture that was inside.

It was a picture of her mama, papa, a much younger George, and baby her being carried in her mamas arms.

"She was right! I do have mamas ears! And oh look, that's the same as Tam Tam's nose. She and Georgie have the same hair too!" Maggie looked at the tiny picture with such love and admiration that he told her she could keep it. She hugged him with excitement and ran to show her older brother that had just stepped off of the carousel.

*

"The squirrel." George popped up out of nowhere beside his father who was staring at the endless stuffed animals option he had to chose from for winning the dart game.

"Squirrel?"

"Yes, she would love it best."

"What made you think I was getting something for Ms.Annabel?"

"I never said it was for her, but there you have it."

Richard and George shared a look.

"It's our secret." George patted his fathers shoulder and walked away.

"Have you decided?" The impatient man running the game said to him.

"Yeah, um, that-that squirrel would do."

*

"If I was a dinosaur-"

"They're extinct." George cut Tam off.

"I know, but if I were one, I'd eat you first."

George flicked a piece of popcorn at her head and she ate it aggressively to show him how she would munch on him.

"Would Margot eat the popcorn or the hot dog?" Their father asked, trying to decide on what he should feed her, he didn't really know what was suitable for her age and he forgot to ask Annabel.

They were all sitting on a picnic table eating lunch.

"I reckon just give her the bun." George said, also having no idea.

"Won't she choke?" Richard asked.

Sam ripped a piece of his hotdog bun off, dipped it in his water and gave it to Margot who happily ate it.

"That could work."

"I'm pretty sure she can eat lots of solid food. Ma-Ms.Annabel doesn't mash anything for her." Maggie said.

"So hotdog." Richard handed Margot just the hotdog with no bun, covered in ketchup and mustard.

Margot happily began to eat it.

None of them knew what they were doing.

Bedtime Stories

The children came back from the carnival, tired and drained from all energy. It was late in the evening when they came back and Annabel was at the door to greet them.

"Let me help you." She grabbed Tam from George who was carrying her and a sleeping Margot.

Sam, Tam and Margot were half awake by the time Annabel finished changing their clothes, taking them to the bathroom and washing them up after their day of fun.

She tucked them all in and was about to turn off the lamp before she got asked to read them a book.

She grabbed one of their favourite books from off the self and sat on the rocking chair to read out loud.

Halfway through, Tam and Margot fell asleep and Sam was about to. He crawled out of his bed and climbed on her lap. He curled himself up and listened to her softly read out loud to him.

Richard limped down the hall to his youngest childrens room to check on them only to find the door already slightly ajar and a dim light coming from it.

He looked inside and his heart and entire body warmed at seeing his son curled up on Annabel's lap while she softly read out loud to him. He understood why Sami saw her as a mother figure. Who wouldn't when she put her heart and soul into taking care of them?

He watched as she closed the book, kissed Sams sleeping head and gently carried him to his bed and tucked him in.

He, for some reason, panicked at the thought of getting caught peering in, although he did nothing wrong. He quickly took a few steps away, turned back, and made it look like he was just walking up to the door.

Annabel gently closed the door after her and turned around only to bump into someone's chest. A hand flew out and steadied her, pulling her close and she placed her hand on it to steady herself. She looked up to see Richard and a light blush spread across her face. She was glad it was semi dark in the hallway and he wouldn't be able to see her red cheeks.

"Are you alright?"

"Yes, thank you for catching me." She stepped away from him.

"How are the kids?" He curled his fingers not holding the cane because he so badly wanted to pull her back to him but stopped himself.

"Sound asleep. They must have really used up all of their energy." She smiled at the thought of the kids laughing and having fun.

"They did, wouldn't sit around for more than two minutes."

"Mr.Pelton I must ask, what did you feed Margot?"

"A hotdog with ketchup and mustard. Why? I shouldn't have right? She's not going to get sick is she?"

She softly giggled and something erupted in his stomach at the melodic sound.

"No, only terribly gassy." She opened the bedroom door and they both peered into it just in time for Margot to let one loose in her sleep.

She giggled again and he chuckled.

"I discovered mustard gets her really gassy and have been avoiding giving it to her like the plague."

"I see, I will keep that in mind."

Silence passed as they looked at each other.

"Right, I also wanted to thank you with Maggie." He blinked and snapped himself out of it.

They began to walk away from the room and further down the hall.

"I was never able to calm her down when her fountain opened up and she was happy and more excited than anyone to be at the carnival."

"Sometimes her emotions and stress get bottled up and then she has a breakdown like that, but that's completely normal for a teenage girl. I remember crying over the silliest things when I was her age."

"Oh yeah? Like what?" He glanced at her with amusement.

"I dropped my ice-cream on the ground and my brother accidentally stepped in it." She laughed at the memory. "I was crying hysterically, but mind you! We only got ice-cream twice a year, so it was very special to me."

Richard laughed and they came to stop in front of her room.

"You didn't get another one?"

"No, my papa couldn't afforded it then. My brother was forced to share his with me, although he really had no fault in me dropping it. Well, this is me."

She opened the door and slipped in. She turned around and looked up at him with a sweet smile.

"Have a good night Mr.Pelton."

"You too."

She shut the door and he opened his mouth to say something more, but closed it. He didn't even give her her squirrel.

A Splash in the Stream

"He's fully recovered, but he might have a slight limp forever." The doctor packed up his bag.

"But he still uses the cane." Annabel walked him to the door with James.

"Yes that's because he might be subconsciously stopping himself from putting his full weight on his leg in fear that it might hurt him. I can't help him there. That's something he has to get over alone."

"Alright. We thank you for your visit." James handed the doctor the money for his visit and closed the door after him.

"Well that's good to hear." Annabel said to James who nodded at her.

"Yes indeed. The children will be happy their father is okay now."

"What did the doctor say?" George walked up to them, book in hand, pencil resting on top of his ear.

"He's all healed up, but he'll have a limp." She said.

"That's wonderful news! We should celebrate. There's a social event we have to attend a week from now, I'll raise a toast for him then."

"Whatever this social event is, I'm not going. I don't like social events. Your siblings and I are going out for a picnic though, would you like to join us?" She picked up Margot that came running in, with Sam and Tam chasing after her.

"I would love to, but school starts soon and I'm trying to get ahead of my peers."

"I see, study hard then."

"Always." He kissed her and Margot's cheek before making his way over to his fathers office.

"I'm ready to go, are you?" Maggie came in with her dress and hat. A picnic box in hand.

"Yes, let's head out."

They set up their picnic a ways away from the house and near the stream.

"Help me keep an eye out on your younger siblings and make sure they don't go close to the stream and decide to jump in." Annabel said as she and Maggie set up the checkered cloth and food.

"Why? Can't you swim?" Maggie asked with amusement.

"No, I actually cannot."

"You could do so many things but cannot swim?"

"Can you swim?"

"Well no, but-"

"Exactly, not everyone ca-"

They were cut off by a high pitched scream.

Annabel's blood ran cold as she turned around to find Tam and Margot at the edge of the stream, looking petrified.

"Sam..." Annabel and Maggie jumped up and ran to the two girls.

Sam was flailing in the water as the stream carried him away.

"Saaaam!" Maggie screamed and was about to jump in after him, but was pulled back by Annabel.

"Let me go!"

"No! You cannot swim and I will not have you drown! Make sure the other two don't jump in." Whiteout a second thought, Annabel took her shoes and dress off. Leaving her in her chemise and drawers. She jumped into the water and went after Sam who was going under far longer than being up.

"No! Mama!" Maggie screamed for Annabel and terror corsed through her veins as she watched her try to make her way to Sam. She grabbed Tam and Margot and ran all the way back to the house to get help.

"Papa! Papa!" She screamed into the air as she neared the house.

Annabel kept her eyes on Sams bobbing head and trained her ears on his screams. She pushed forward and called out to him. She was in no way actually swimming, just trying her best.

Sam looked at her with pleading eyes.

"Mama! Help me Mama!" He reached a hand out to her and then he completely submerged.

Annabel pulled him up by the shirt and struggled to keep the both of them floating. Sam clung onto her neck and she kicked against the water current and dragged the two of them to safety.

Richard sat up straight when he thought he heard someone scream his name.

"Did you hear that?" He asked George.

"No. What did you-"

"Papa! Help Papa!" Maggie's scream was faint but still very clear.

Both men jumped up and ran out the door to see the three girls in hysterics.

Richard ran the rest of the way to them and held Maggie by her shoulders. He completely disregarded the cane and was able to over come his mental block of walking without it.

"What is it? What's wrong?"

Maggie was crying too hard to make a coherent sentence.

"Mama! It's mama and Sam!" Tam cried out.

"What's wrong with mama? Where is she?" Richard looked around but didn't find the two of them. "Dammit! Speak Maggie!"

"Sami fell into the stream and Mama jumped after him. But mama-mama, she can't swim. Papa they're both going to drown! Do something! Save them papa!"

"Take them inside." He said to George and immediately took off to the stream.

He took off his blazer and tossed it to the side as he ran. His waistcoat and button up soon following. He kicked his shoes off and stumbled but managed to get his socks off.

The stream was just ahead and he could see where they set up their picnic and he ran even faster.

"SAAM! ANNABEL!" He screamed when he reached the stream and ran along it to look for them.

"Mama!"

He heard Sam scream and pushed forward.

Sam stood at the edge of the stream screaming as he saw Annabel get swept away and lose her hold on the edge. She could barely keep her head up and soon went fully underneath.

Richard dived into the freezing water and swam underneath, keeping his eyes peeled open and on the drowning figure, yards in front of him.

He pushed himself hard and reached forward, straining to get a hold of her. His fingers brushed along the fabric of her clothes and he was able to wrap his fingers around the collar of her chemise.

He made a break for the surface and gasped for air.

"Come on. I got you Annabel." He pushed through the current with one hand while the other was holding on to her.

Sam ran up to them and tried his best to pull her up when his father was pushing her out of the water before him.

Richard pulled himself up and fell beside her, still breathing heavily from the swimming and running.

"Annabel? Annie?" He asked, turning his head to the side to look at her, but she wasn't responding.

He got up and laid her on her back properly.

"Wake up mama!" Sam cried and shook her shoulders, but she still didn't open her eyes.

Richard put his hands over her chest and began chest compressions.

"Fuck, you have to get up Annabel." He continued to try and revive her in a state of complete panic.

George, James, and a few horse handlers ran down the field and came to a stop when they saw Richard trying chest compressions on Annabel.

"Mama!" George ran forward and fell on his knees beside his father and Sam.

One of the handlers picked up Sam and wrapped him in a blanket.

After a few more tries Annabel coughed up water and began taking in big gulps of air.

"Of thank god." Richard pulled her close and sighed in relief. His shoulders dropped and he rested his chin on top of her head.

"Sam. Where's Sam?" She looked around trying to make sense of the situation while Sam wiggled out of the man's hold and launched himself into her lap.

"Oh thank god you're okay." She wrapped her arms around and a few tears ran down her face. "I was so scared I'd lose you." She kissed the top of his head and relaxed in the arms of Richard.

George wrapped his arms around all of them and she kissed the top of his head as well.

"Let's never do that again shall we?" Richard chuckled and she looked up at him and smiled.

"Sounds like a plan."

Dinner With the Von Eckermans

"**W**hy did you invite the Von Eckermans over to dinner when mama still isn't feeling well?" Maggie marched with her father around the house.

"Not just them. A few others as well." George said walking past them.

"You really think this is a good idea papa?" Maggie continued to pester her father with questions.

"Master Richard, I need someone to do a quick grocery run. I'm missing a few ingredients for all the stuff I have to cook." Samantha said and took his other flank.

"Would you like me to invite the guests into the dining area first or into the entertainment room?" James walked by them.

"Papa!" Margot ran up to him and asked to be held and he picked her up.

"Sorry, I'm trying to get her changed but she keeps running away." Annabel took her from him and looked him up and down. "Are you going to wear that for this evening?"

"Is there a problem with it?" He asked, concerned that he didn't look good.

"Not at all, but I think it would be better if you went with the navy one. Change things up a little."

"You think so?" He looked down at the black tux he was wearing.

"I mean it's up to you."

"Navy it is then." He started making his way to his room.

"Master what about the groceries?"

"And which room should I bring everyone into first?"

"I still don't think this is a good idea."

"Everyone! This isn't the first time we've hosted a large dinner. You know what to do. Samantha get the driver to pick up what you need, quickly. James, the entertainment room. And Maggie, I don't want to hear it."

"But mama-"

"Mama! Mama looks fine. Plus, she'll be looking after the twins and Margot after they're done greeting everyone. She'll be up in the playroom all evening. You can go and sit there with here after socializing and dinner. Understand?"

"Yes papa."

Annabel finished getting the twins and Margot dressed and she was now working on styling their hair.

"Sam, no Sam! It looks good like that, why would you ruin it? Come here so I could brush it again."

"But mama you're not done with my hair." Tam pouted.

"Right, sorry. Sam, here's your brush. Please fix your hair." And she went back to putting Tam's hair up in a sleek bun.

"Annabel." Richard called from the door. He was focusing on his cuflinks and just couldn't get them to cooperate.

"Come here." She motioned for him to come closer and she got up from Tams bed and meet him halfway across the room.

"Is this one better?" He asked and closely studied her face as she grabbed his arm and got the buttons to work. He tucked a loose piece of hair from her braid behind her ear and glided his thumb over her cheek. She momentarily froze but continued doing up the buttons. Ignoring the fact that he was now tracing her eyebrow and jawline.

"Much, now, let me just," she smoothed down the lapels on his suit and straightened his bow tie. "there."

"Thank you."

She looked up into his blue eyes and lightly flushed.

"Right, well, Tam is all ready. I have to fix Sam's hair and Margot is almost done." She stepped away and went to brush Sam's hair.

"Are you sure you don't want to join us?" He asked, wanting to continue with the conversation and stay in her presence longer.

"I am not the daughter of aristocrats, so I wouldn't know how to act in such a big and fancy social situation, I wasn't trained. Plus, all I have is very simple work dresses that will not suit this event. I will only be an embarrassment. I am also still not feeling my best from after that splash in the stream." She got up off her knees from doing Sam's hair and turned around to get to Margot, but Richard stepped in her way and she put her hand up on his chest so she wouldn't fully smack into him and he immediately put his hands on her waist.

"You're not an embarrassment and you'll look good in anything you wear. You could wear some of Marries clothes that are in the boxes. And you know I don't care about the different classes, else I would have hired someone of the upper class to look after our kids." He dipped his head slightly to show her his sincerity.

"Your flattery won't work on me Mr.Pelton, and wearing your late wife's clothes doesn't sit right with me. And you might not feel embarrassed but people talk. And it's not right for your children's nanny to attend these social events. Your family will be judged and mocked and I will not have that."

She made a move to side step him but he held onto her tighter and held her in place.

"Let go please."

But he didn't, he pulled her slightly closer and her breathing hitched.

"But what people-"

"You're a family I care about and I don't want to ruin your image. I'll be staying up here looking after the twins and Margot so they don't bother the guests too much, now excuse me Sir, but I haven't finished Margot's hair."

He let go and she went to Margot. Only then did he realise that he said our kids.

*

The twins and Margot were sent up to the playroom when it was time for dinner. Annabel sat and fed Margot when one of the maids brought food up for them ; the twins were able to eat by themselves.

"I need help washing my face!" Tam called from down the hall in the washroom.

"You two stay right there. I'm going to go help your sister." She got one of the maids running down the hallway to temporarily babysit them.

"You didn't have to make such a big mess Tam Tam." Annabel sighed and cleaned the spilt water and washed her face. "Don't worry about the water on your dress, it will dry."

They walked back to the playroom to find a very frantic maid.

"What's wrong?"

"It's Margot. I turned my back for one second and now she's gone. I don't know where she is!"

"She's missing?" Annabel groaned. "Stay here and look after the twins while I go look for her. I trust you won't lose them too?"

The maid nodded and Annabel searched the rooms on the top floor but found nothing.

"Please don't be in the dinning room, please don't be in the dinning room." She glanced in the dinning room where all the guests were seated and scanned the floor for tiny feet, but found none. "Thank god."

An overly obnoxious laugh caught her attention and she saw a blond, red liped women was sitting next to Richard and laughing very loudly.

"You are even funnier than what my father said!" She placed a hand on his arm that was resting on the table and for some reason that didn't sit well with Annabel.

She wanted nothing more than to rip the women's arm off of Richard and have him place them around her again.

Richard caught her eye and lit up at seeing her, completely forgetting about the women beside him.

"Excuse me, I'll be back shortly." He got up from his seat, eyes never leaving Annabel even when she sneaked away towards the library.

"What are you doing?" He whispered as to not startle her. She was looking behind the curtains and under the tables in the dark, unlit library. The only light provided was coming in from the moon. He didn't expect her to come down at all.

"Looking for Margot." She whispered back and continued to look.

"She's missing?"

"Ran away the second I wasn't in the room." She grumbled.

Richard helped look for Margot, they even began bribing her.

"Come out Margot, I'll give you some chocolate." He made kissing noises like he was calling a puppy.

"She's not going to come if you keep making those horrid noises!" Annabel whisper shouted at him.

"Yes she will, you just watch!" He whisper shouted back

"What are you two doing?" A female voice said accusingly and the lights were turned on.

Both Annabel and Richard banged their head from under the table they were looking in, in surprise.

"Who are you?" It was the women from earlier and she looked Annabel up and down in a very judgmental way.

"This is Annabel. My children's nanny and we're looking for Margot." Richard was clueless to the hateful glare being thrown Annabel's way that turned into a soft one once the women knew she was only just a nanny and not a threat of any kind.

"I see. Well, I am Rebeca Von Eckerman, pleasure to meet you."

"Like wise."

"Richard, let's go back to the table of unfinished food. You can't have us wait too long. You are the host." She gave Richard a sweet smile, grabbed his arm and tugged him towards the door.

"But my daughter, she's -"

"Well that's what the nanny is for, isn't she? She can look for your daughter herself. That is what you pay her for after all."

They walked out of the library and Richard gave Annabel an apologetic smile.

There was nothing wrong with what Rebeca just said. It was all true. But the way she said it humiliated Annabel a little bit. She loved her job and looking after the children, and she would even continue to look after them if Richard stopped paying her, because she loves them so much. So she doesn't understand why she felt humiliated and slightly embarrassed. There's nothing embarrassing about looking after kids.

She made her way back to the foyer in hopes of finding Margot roaming there.

"Excuse me Miss. Would you happen to know where the washroom is?" A well put together man that looked only a year or two older than her, spoke up.

"You'd find them down that hallway, second door to your right." She motioned to the hallway and was about to head back upstairs when he stopped her again.

"Miss, you don't, you don't work here do you? I mean you're not dressed like the maids." He took a few steps forward so he was standing in front of her.

"I do actually. I look after the children. In fact, I'm looking for one of them right now." She took a slight step back and began to turn when he spoke up yet again.

"I could help you look if you'd let me?"

"That's quite all right. I can look for her myself. Didn't you have to use the washroom?"

"Yes of course. I'll see you around Miss..."

"Annabel, my name is Annabel."

"I'll see you around Miss. Annabel." He took her hand, bent over and placed a kiss.

They both jumped in slight surprise at the sound of a high pitched feminine scream coming from the dinning room.

They shared a concerned look with each other and were about to make their way over when a fuming Rebeca marched out of the dining room. Dress ruined with food that had spilled all over.

She saw Annabel standing there and made her way over to her.

"It's all your fault!"

She did something no one expected. Not Annabel, not the man beside her, not Richard that had followed her while carrying Margot or the guests that followed behind to see the drama.

Rebeca slapped Annabel. Hard.

"What was that for?" The man stepped between the two women and held his hand out to stop any advances coming from Rebeca, slightly pushing her back.

"You're a horrible caretaker and you don't teach the kids any manners!" She then turned around to Richard and addressed him. "You listen well Richard, you get rid of her immediately and I will find you the best nanny there ever is. If this women continues to look after your kids, they will all turn into savages!"

Annabel brought a hand up to her burning cheek and she couldn't help but wonder how pathetic she looked in the eyes of the children that were watching the interaction.

Maggie's eyes were open wide and George's jaw hung open while Margot began to cry at seeing Annabel get slapped. She wiggled so much in her fathers hold, that he set her down and she ran to Annabel and hugged her legs. Sam and Tam were watching at the top of the stairs and tears gathered in their eyes.

"I may not be the best nanny on earth but I care for these children and am trying to help raise them in a way that will make them successful and beneficial to society. Margot is only a three year old and is prone to make mistakes and cause accidents. I apologise on her behalf for ruining your dress and I'm sure that in your big, kind heart you will find it in you to forgive the child."

She turned to look at Richard with slight hurt eyes at not having him stand up for her in the slightest.

"Since Margot has been found I'll head back upstairs and get the children ready for bed. I also hope you don't mind if I retire early tonight, Mr.Pel ton?"

"Y-yeah of course." It hurt his heart to see her begin to tear up like that and that he didn't do anything to make her feel better. He wanted nothing more than to swoop her in his arms in a tight hug and brush the tears away, but he couldn't, it wasn't appropriate. Not now where there was watchful eyes and not ever, because she was only his children's nanny.

"Good night everyone." She picked up Margot and she immediately calmed down and snuggled into her neck.

Annabel turned around and headed upstairs. That seemed to conclude the drama and people started to make their way back to the dinning room.

Samantha handed Maggie a bag of ice and she ran after Annabel.

"Well done father. You didn't stand up for mama and you let Ms.Eckerman hurt her. Who does that to the women they love?" George harshly whispered to him.

Did he though?

Did he love her?

He couldn't possibly.

Even if he did, he couldn't allow himself to.

He had to do something to get his mind and heart off of her.

*

"Annabel, can I come in?"

Silence even though he knew she was awake because of the dim light coming underneath her door.

"Please?"

She unlocked the door and went back to her book on the couch.

He took that as an invitation to come in and opened the door and walked in.

"I wanted to apologise."

"What for?" She didn't look up from her book.

He sighed heavily, looked at the freezing ice bag in his hand and tossed it to her. Annabel wasn't looking and saw it in her peripheral vision at the last second before it made contact with her already stinging cheek.

"I'm sorry! I'm sorry! I'm awfully sorry." Richard rushed forward and sat right beside her on the couch. One leg underneath him as he faced her and picked up the bag. "I didn't mean to hurt you even more. I thought you might have seen it."

He gently pressed the ice to her cheek and she lifted her hand and rested it on top of his to have him let go so she could hold the bag in place, but he didn't remove his and instead, he pulled his thumb from under her hand and rested it on top of hers.

"I brought you something. Hopefully it will help make you forgive me easier." He nudged the squirrel toy towards her and her eyes lit up and that brought joy to him.

She removed her hand, set the book aside and picked up the squirrel.

"You got this for me?"

He brought his hand, holding the ice, down and scratched the back of his neck in slight embarrassment.

"A while ago actually. It was when I took the kids to the carnival. I won it at a dart game. Never got a chance to give it to you until now."

"It's very kind of you, thank you, although I still don't know what you're apologising for."

"For not standing up for you and letting her talk to you like that. And for letting her drag me away while we were looking for Margot."

"You're not responsible for how people act and what they say."

"But I still should have said something. She said hurtful things and said that you didn't know what you were doing. It's not true. And Margot didn't do it on purpose, it was on accident, so it's not even a behavioural problem. She was wrong for saying that."

He sat closer and took both her hands in his.

"I'm really sorry."

"It's alright, I forgive you, although I still fail to see how this is your fault. You're not obliged to stand up for me. I think I handled myself pretty well, don't you think Mr.Pelton?"

"Richard, please."

"I can't, it's unprofessional."

"Then when we're alone. We don't have to be so formal with each other."

"Oh, I don't think we even are that formal sometimes." She looked down at their hands pointedly and pulled them away.

He looked down at his hands that were just holding hers and smiled.

"I guess not."

The Engagement

"Ms. Von Eckerman is here, Master Richard." James led the lady into the tea room where they had their tea and breakfast.

The tea room was very bright with the amount of sunlight coming in from the windows. Three of its walls were glass that peered over the field where the horses grazed in.

The children had a separate, bigger, round table than their father, who had a table for two and always sat alone. Occasionally, he would force Annabel to sit and eat with him, insisting that Margot didn't need help with eating all the time and that she herself should be eating meals during their proper time and not later because she was looking after them. Meals first.

This time, Annabel was feeding Margot, mostly teaching her how to eat by herself, so she has created some sort of mess and Richard was at his table alone.

Rebeca Von Eckerman stepped into the sunlit room, eyes surveying the place. A look of slight irritation crossed her face when she saw Annabel and the mess Margot was creating.

"Good morning Richard. I thought I told you to fire her and that I was going to find you someone better?" She walked up to Richard, her heels clicking on the ground.

He got up and kissed her cheek in greeting, one hand on her hips.

Maggie and George shared a disgusted look.

"Ms.Annabel will not be leaving. She looks after the children with excellent care and love. I won't hear another word about finding a replacement for her." He sat back down and went back to reading the newspaper.

"Alright, but don't make me say I told you so." She sat down in the other chair and when Richard put down the newspaper, they began small talk.

"What do you thinks gotten into papa?" Maggie whispered to George.

"Idiocy and stupidity if you ask me." He whispered back.

"George!" Maggie said in whispered surprise.

"It's true. He could have the best women in the world right here but he doesn't want to believe his own heart." He said even more quietly so Annabel couldn't hear.

They both watched her slightly laugh when Margot flicked food at her face.

"True, an idiot indeed." Maggie sighed and they went back to eating their breakfast with solemn expressions.

*

"Papa, I thought you and I were going to go over some paper work?" George asked his father who was grabbing his Homburg hat and buttoning up his blazer.

"After I take Ms.Eckerman in town to do some shopping." Richard held his arm out for Rebeca and she placed her hand on it.

"We'll see you children after noon." She said, standing closer to Richard than necessary.

"Be good to Annabel." Richard said opening the door and closing it after them when they stepped out.

"Ooo I'm going to take RebeCa out shopping! Ooo she's hanging off of me and pressing her breasts on my arm. Ooo I'm going to shower her with gifts!" Maggie said in a mocking higher than her normal voice tone.

George sniggered.

"Don't say that out loud in fear she might hear you and slap you." He said and Maggie burst out laughing.

"Like papa would let her. She'll be kicked out as soon as she does." She giggled at the thought but George frowned.

"Yeah, but he didn't do anything when she hit mama."

"Right."

*

Moments after they were done with their lunch, someone was at the door.

"Annabel. It's for you." James said, walking into the dining room were she was pulling Margot out of her high chair and everyone was getting up.

"For me?"

She and George shared a look and they both made their way to the front door, the curious kids coming after them.

"Ms.Annabel, so lovely to see you." The man from last night was at the door with a bouquet of flowers in his hand.

"These are..."

"For you, yes." He handed her the flowers and flashed her a million dollar smile.

"Oh, um, thank you." She held the flowers close to her, not really sure what to do.

"Mr.Fredrick, my father is not here right now. Please come back at another time." George stepped forward.

"I'm actually not here to see your father, but Ms.Annabel. I was wondering if you'd like to go for an afternoon stroll with me?"

"But I hardly know you."

"Which is why we'll get to know each other. Just a quick stroll, we'll be back before the sun sets."

She looked at George for help, but an idea was forming in his mind and he gave her an encouraging nod.

"Even Pelton junior doesn't mind." Fredrick said to persuade her more.

"I'm confused as to why you'd want to take a stroll with someone of a much lower social class than yourself."

"It does not bother me and should not be the deciding factor in my decision with who I want to court."

She was slightly surprised at the use of the old term for dating, it wasn't used too much like a few years ago.

"C-court!? Don't you think-"

"It's just a stroll Ms.Annabel, nothing serious." He gave her a soft smile.

"She'll be ready in a few minutes." Maggie said. She grabbed Annabel by the hand and ran up the stairs with her.

"I'll be waiting here then." He said smiling from ear to ear.

Both George and Fredrick watched as she ran up the stairs.

"So where is your father?" He turned his head towards George.

"Taking your obnoxious sister out on a date."

"Half sister."

"Still your sister."

Fredrick and George both sighed at the same time and went to sit on the couch in the foyer. A maid took the younger kids away.

"I feel bad for him. He has to deal with her. She's a lot of maintenance." Fredrick lifted his arms and rested them on the back of the couch.

"I will never get married to a person like her."

"Good for you Pelton."

They went quiet for a few seconds before George turned his head to look at Fredrick.

"So, my nanny?"

"She's a wonderful person. Did you see her two nights ago? She got my heart racing when she calmly stood up for herself."

George hummed a response and they both turned to look at the stairs when Annabel and Maggie came down them. She was wearing a light blue simple dress and her hair was in a low bun with a hat on to keep the sun out of her eyes. Light powder and blush adorned her face giving her a natural flushed look.

George smiled at how pretty his mama looked and Fredricks heart beat faster at seeing her simple, elegant, beauty.

"You look beautiful." He said approaching the stairs and held his arm out when she reached the last step.

"You're being too kind." She placed her hand on his arm and they made their way to the door.

"Take care of your younger siblings and yourselves while I'm gone." She said to George and Maggie who nodded at her and ushered them out the door.

"Do you think it will work?" Maggie asked George when the two adults were out the door.

"It definitely will."

With Annabel seeing another man, they hoped their father got jealous and admit his feelings.

*

"We're home!" Richard called out and heard the sound of pounding feet coming from the top floor. His children came rushing down the stairs and their eyes gawked at the amount of bags and boxes being carried in.

"What's all this papa?" Sam asked as Richard picked him up.

"Stuff I got for Rebeca and the lot of you." He grinned and kissed Sam's cheek.

"Rebeca? Just this morning you were calling her Ms.Von Eckerman." Maggie protested and gave Rebeca a nasty glare which's she responded to with a smug smile.

"Yes well, your father and I have an announcement to make." She took Richards hand and intertwined their fingers.

"Yes we do," Richard looked around but couldn't find her, "where's Annabel? It would be best to say this announcement to everyone at the same time."

"Who cares? Her opinion doesn't matter here, she works for you." Rebeca sweetly smiled up at him.

"Yes, but-"

"Your papa and I are engaged!" She excitedly said and took of her elbow long glove to reveal a diamond ring.

Everyone in the house froze.

The maids and the horse handlers bringing in the boxes, James directing them to the living room, Samantha who had just came out of the kitchen with a plate of warm cookies for the kids before bed, which she dropped, and the kids, they had the most heartbroken, shocked looks on their faces.

"George." Maggie's lower lip trembled and she clutched her older brothers hand.

Richard didn't expect this reaction from his kids. He thought that they might be happy for him, but they all looked like they were on the verge of tears. Only George was the most put together as he gathered Tam in his arms and handed Margot to Maggie. He took Sam from his arms and looked at him with a blank expression.

"We wish you happiness in this marriage that we do not agree to, but our opinions do not matter. I hope this wasn't an impulsive decision father. Good night."

They went up the stairs together and Richard sighed in defeat.

"I apologise, I really thought they might be happy."

"It's alright, I understand where they are coming from. They're not ready to see another women other than their mother by your side. It will take them time to adjust." She patted Richards arm and he smiled down at her.

"Thank you for understanding. It's getting late now, I'll get my driver to get you home safely. We have a big day tomorrow with you moving in."

"Yes we do, don't we?" She leaned up and kissed his cheek before heading out. He couldn't help but wipe it off.

Richard immediately went on a hunt to find Annabel. He searched everywhere he thought she was, the library, the kitchen, the living room, her room, he knocked on bathroom doors and checked the children's room in case she was tucking them in, but they were already asleep. He even visited the barn and that's where Phil told him that she had headed out since the afternoon.

He nervously paced the foyer waiting for her to return home. He even placed a chair in front of the door to sit on and wait, but he was too fidgety and anxious for her safety. What if she got lost? What if she fell and hurt herself and couldn't get back up? What if she feel in the stream again? What if someone took advantage of her in the dark?

Ideas that made him even more panicked raced through his head. He kept checking his pocket watch and when she hasn't shown up for half an hour he decided that he was going to go out and look for her. Where? He didn't know, but he couldn't just sit in the house with the possibility of her being in danger out there.

He turned on his heels and went to grab his blazer that he disregarded on the chair, and just as he was about to slip it on, the front door opened up and she walked in with a bright smile on her face.

Relief washed over him and he dropped the blazer on the ground and made his way over to her.

Annabel thanked Fredrick for a wonderful time, a smile adorned her face, and when she shut the door she was aggressively turned around by her shoulders and pulled into a bone crushing, protective hug.

Richard had one arm vertically pressed on her back, pulling her close, and the other one in her hair.

"You had me so worried."

Suddenly, he let go of her in irritation and went back to pacing back and forth, a hand running through his hair.

"Richard, are you all right? You seem concerned." She asked, concerned about the sudden switch in his mood.

"Concerned? Me? Am I concerned? What an absurd question. Of course I was concerned!" He raised his voice and she slightly flinched.

"You've been gone since the afternoon! You left the kids all alone! And you come back late at evening! How could I not be concerned and mad!?"

"Well the kids said-"

"I don't CARE what the kids said!" He shouted and looked at her. "You left them alone and they could have gotten hurt! They were left without anyone to take care of them! How could you just leave them like that?"

"If you would just let me talk you would know I didn't leave on my own free will! Your kids forced me to go out with Mr.Fredrick. I didn't leave them unattended! I had them bake cookies with Samantha, play games with Phil, and attend to their studies with James. They were supervised at all times. And you! You should have a little more faith in your kids! George and Maggie are all grown up and can handle a little responsibility and looking after their siblings for a few hours."

"But you left for far longer than a few hours! That's not being responsible." He took a deep breath and held his own fingers behind his back and stood sideways to her. "Maybe Rebeca was right."

"What?"

"Her and I got engaged and are planning to get married. She'll be here a lot more often and will be able to take care of the kids without your assistance."

"What are you saying?"

He turned his head towards her but it was tilted down to the ground.

"I'm saying that your services are no longer required." He looked up with a mean glare. "Leave."

"You don't mean that. Richard you don't-"

"We don't need you here any longer."

Tears pooled in Annabel's eyes and they trickled down her face.

She rushed up the stairs, past the children who were watching what was happening and into her room were she threw open her bag and shoved the very little amount of clothes she had, in it. She glanced at the squirrel stuffed animal on her bed, more tears running down her face and she kept it there.

She shut the suitcase and picked it up, heading out.

"You listen well children. You have to be good to your father and Ms.Von Eckerman. Don't cause trouble and stay on top of all your studies. You understand?" She held Maggie's crying face in her hands. "You're such a beautiful girl Maggie, I'm sure you'll be able to achieve anything you set your mind to."

She tucked her hair behind her ears and kissed her forehead.

"You're such a good boy Georgie, you keep pursuing your dreams. I want to one day open the papers and see your name front and center for having designed the best thing in the world."

She kissed his cheek and kneeled down in front of the twins.

"If you keep crying you'll make me sad. Sami, look after Tami. And you make sure your brother doesn't do anything too dangerous." She kissed their heads. She kissed Margot's cheek, picked up her bag and rushed down the stairs and out the door, without sparing Richard a glance.

He slumped on the chair, a hand covering his mouth in shock at what he had just done and a single tear rolled down his face.

"Noo!" George's voice broke in the end. "No Mama don't go!"

He has registered what has happened and ran down the stairs, aggressively opening the front door and running out into the now pouring sky.

"Mamaaa!" He screamed for her, tears getting mixed with rain.

"George." She placed her bag down and turned around in time to catch him throwing himself at her.

"Mama don't go, please." He clung to her and put his face in the crook of her neck.

"You know it isn't up to me whether I stay or go. You have to respect your father's decision."

She pulled back and looked up into his face, she placed a hand on his cheek and he leaned into it.

"You can't leave us alone with her. You can't. You have to stay with us. You haven't finished taking care of us. Sam and Tam are going to year 2 in less than a month, and Margot, she's going to go in hysterics once she realises you're not coming back. A-and you know Maggie is going to be heartbroken and depressed and relapse to her bad behavior. And me. You'll be leaving me. I can't lose my mama a second time. I-I can't."

"George, Georgie you have to listen to me." She put her other hand on his face and smiled at him. "You're a strong young man George, and me leaving, a nobody, a nanny, shouldn't bring you down."

"But you're not a nobody! You're my mama!"

"George, I wish I could stay. I really do." Tears rolled down her cheek. "But your papa has made his decision and this was bound to happen sooner or later. Look after your siblings for me, would you?"

Maggie ran down the stairs with a tear streaked face.

"Mama!"

Richard held her back from going in the rain and she kicked and lashed out.

"Let me go! Let me go! I have to go see mama!"

"No! It's raining outside and you're in your nightgown."

"I don't care! Let me go!" She kicked and lashed out even harder. "I hate you! I hate you I hate you I hate you!" She screamed at her father.

He let go in surprise and shock and she dashed out the door.

"Mama!"

Annabel looked up to see Maggie running down the front steps.

"I have to go George. Good bye."

"No, good byes are forever. You always said good byes are forever, you can't say good bye. You can't!"

She picked up her luggage and continued on her way to the city a few miles away, leaving her life with the Peltons behind.

No Mama

"Richard, you will never believe what my brother told me." Rebeca said, first thing when she walked in the house.

"And what would that be?" He said, not in a very particularly good mood for her overly cheerful and somewhat fake attitude.

"He took your childrens nanny out for a stroll! Can you believe that?" She snapped her fan closed. "I mean, what does he see in that horrid creature?"

A nerve bulged in his temple and he bit his tongue from saying something harsh and kicking her out of the house.

He just set the morning paper down on the table and made his way to the library without saying a single world.

"Has he grown so desperate to find a women that he would lower his standards so much? He's not even that bad looking. He could get any girl he wanted from the upper and noble class, what was he thinking?" Rebeca followed Richard into the library, not picking up on his anger.

"I'll have you know! Mama is more beautiful than you, you old ugly hag!" Sam screamed at her from the top of the stairs.

"I'll ignore what he said because he looks really upset, but you really should fire her if this is the vocabulary she is teaching them." She took a seat across from him and poked one of the books stacked up.

"I'll have you know. I fired her last night." He flipped through the book he was reading, not actually reading anything, but hoping this would get her to stop talking to him.

"Excellent news! I'll find you a new one immediately!" She excitedly got up and was about to hurry out of the library.

"Actually. Actually I was thinking to not bring them a nanny. I thought since you will be their step mother you might want to spend time with them and get to know them better." He slammed his book shut and placed it on the table.

"O-oh, what a wonderful idea." Her lower eye lid trembled at the thought of taking care of children.

*

An entire month passed without Annabel in the Pelton household and everyone has been miserable.

Margot would occasionally call out at night for her while she was sleeping. The twins grew more and more stubborn with everything. Maggie was getting snappy and more detached. George immersed himself in his studies with the start of school and took every opportunity he got to not be home. He was either studying in the public library in the city or out with his friends and he alway came home late and sometimes drunk. He found out that liquor was a great way to numb the pain and nothing stopped him from having it since he was legal now.

And Richard, Richard had many restless nights, tossing and turning. All day his mind would be plagued with the thought of one person, and during the night, her tear stained face would haunt him. It would get his chest all tight and he would begin to choke up at being the reason behind the tears.

Not that Annabel has been doing any better than all of them. She found a new job in the city for another family that weren't as nice as the Pelton's. They were rude and always made her feel bad that she was from a lower, working class. The head of the house, Old Mr.Wilton, has been sick and bed ridden for a very long time and his children and wife are just waiting for him to die so they could inherit all his land and money, not that they haven't been spending it carelessly on useless items. The only good thing that has come out of working for the Wilton's was that they refused Annabel to be working for them in such old ragged dresses. Their eldest daughter, Tiffany, also the only kind person in the household, took her shopping for new dresses, although fairly simple, but still new, and Annabel was grateful. They also forget when her pay day is, so they end up paying her on random days, sometimes even double, so Annabel took it as their way of apologising for being a snobby rich family.

She missed the Pelton children dearly, more than anything, even Richard, and the house staff. She constantly wondered how they were doing and her ears always perked up when Tiffany talks about how gorgeous Mr.Pelton and Ms.Von Eckerman were in the recent social gatherings and events she's been to, and how truly sad it is that he hasn't noticed her. She quickly got over her sadness when she remembered that he had an 18 year old so, George, and she didn't care that he was five years younger than her.

"And oh you should have seen her dress Annabel, it was just the most wonderful thing, it fit her like a glove I tell you." Tiffany hugged her pillow close to her chest with a dreamy expression on her face. "Richard Pelton is one lucky man to have her."

"I'm sure he is." Annabel gritted her teeth and continued picking up the clothes from off of the ground.

"You must come with me next time. I'll doll you up and everything. You can't live without seeing how beautiful the two couple are."

"I don't think that's a good idea Tiff. I'm rather busy working."

"But you can take a day off you know? I'll tell mama that I need you there with me to help me out, she won't say no. You also have to see George. For an eighteen year old he is quite handsome."

Annabel scrunched her nose at someone thinking about George in a romantic manner. She stood up and put her hands on her hips. She studied Tiffany.

In the month she's known her, she's been wonderful. She's well educated and a proper fine lady. She could see her and George getting along fine. The only thing that's a little off was the that she was older. Frankly, Annabel thinks it's fine, and hopes George does too.

"On a scale of one to ten, how badly do you want to meet George Pelton?"

"Oh, one hundred." Tiffany blushed at the thought of meeting him.

"So, would you like me to introduce you to him?"

"You know him!?" Tiffany bounced up on her knees and stared at her wide eyed.

"I worked for them Tiffany. I've already seen Mr.Pelton and Ms. Von Eckerman together." Annabel smiled at the girls excitement, but it soon turned into a sad smile.

"Wait, why are you sad?" Tiffany patted her bed, an invitation for Annabel.

"I just really miss them. They are wonderful people and I wish I didn't leave the way I did. I wish it was on better circumstances that I left."

"What happened?" Tiffany put an arm around Annabel and pulled her head to rest on her shoulders.

"I don't even know. Except the children might hate me now."

"I doubt anyone can hate you Annie. You're too kind."

"Say that to Rebeca." She grumbled.

"Von Eckerman? What did she do?"

"Let's just say she's not as nice as she looks. Now, I have to go finish your siblings rooms and see how they are doing."

"Alright, but now you have to come with me this Friday. No excuses. I'm going to make you the prettiest woman in the room and make Mr.Pelton regret whatever he did to you."

"I'll go with you, on one condition. I don't like to dress too fancy, so something simple will suffice."

"We'll see."

Dress Shopping

"No, not that one. Or that one. This one's too puffy for my liking. Why in the world would I want to wear an orange dress? Tiff, you have horrible taste." Annabel groaned as they looked at dress options and inspirations.

"Oh hush, I know what I'm doing."

They looked through more fabric and dresses.

"Tiffany! Look at this colour. Isn't it just wonderful?" Annabel held a piece of very light green fabric out.

"Yes! This is the one." Tiffany gushed over it and they took it to the seamstress in the back. She had already taken both girls measurements and promised to get the dresses done before Friday, in time for the party.

"George, be a dear and help me pick out a colour your father would like on me." The door dinged and in walked two other customers.

Tiffany and Annabel shared a look.

"You really don't know how much I appreciate you coming along with me." Rebeca Von Eckerman said.

"Oh I do, you keep saying it. And it's not like you forced me to come in here or anything."

Annabel's heart skipped a beat at hearing George's voice. She missed her son more than words could say.

Tiffany grabbed her hand and hurriedly came out from the back and went to a section of fabrics, pretending to look through them.

"He's here." She hissed to Annabel.

"I know."

Tiffany quickly glanced at Annabel and did a double take when she noticed the tears in her eyes. A single one rolled down her face.

"Oh, Annabel." She whispered and brushed the tear away.

George walked around a rack of fabrics, bored and unamused that he was forced to help Rebeca dress shop for a party this Friday. He saw two women looking through the fabrics. One of them he noticed was Tiffany Wilton, a very pretty, well put together lady and the other, the other... it felt like his heart dropped all the way down to his stomach and his breathing hitched.

There's no possible way.

He took a shaky step forward, and another.

"M-mama?"

Annabel turned around, a shaky smile on her lips.

"Hello Georgie."

He rushed forward and she met him with open arms.

He wrapped his arms around her and breathed her scent in. Tears rolled down his face as he hugged her tight.

"It's really you?" He pulled back and he studied her face, his eyes jumping back and forth from looking at one eye, to the other.

"It is." She let out an airy laugh and brought her hands up to his face, brushing the tears away.

"Where have you been all this time? Why didn't you come visit?"

"Do you really think your papa would like it if I just showed up to visit? I'm just a nanny. It's not acce-"

"You're not just a nanny! You're our mama. We've been miserable without you. Even papa. He barely gets any sleep. Please come back. He regrets shouting at you. He won't mind it if you come back. So please. We need you."

"George," she sighed and stepped to the side. "this is Tiffany Wilton. I work for the Wilton's now."

It hurt her to know that they haven't been doing well. She wanted to go back and help them, but even if George said that Richard regrets everything he said and didn't mean it, it's not coming out of Richards mouth. She doesn't know that he actually does regret what he said and that he actually didn't mean any of it.

George wiped the excess tears and held his hand out and gave her hand a polite shake.

"Pleasure to meet you Ms.Wilton. Please excuse the tears, I haven't seen my mama in-"

"I know. I'm really happy you two have finally reunited. Annabel always looks like she's slightly in a depressed mood, I've never seen her look happier."

"Then please let her come back to us. All your siblings are over ten, mine aren't. They need their mama." He pleaded with her.

"That's not up for me to decide. It's up to her." She nodded towards Annabel.

"Mama." George looked at her with pleading eyes and held her hands. "Say you'll come home."

"That's up for your papa to decide."

"Well papa can't live without you anyways. So that will be easy to take care of."

"Don't be ridiculous George."

"I'm not! You should see him. He always walks into your room and just paces, sometimes we even find him reading a book there. The squirrel you left behind, he took it and placed it on his vanity and your hair ribbon that you dropped from that race with Maggie, it's always in his pocket where he never takes his hand out. Maggie walked in on him in his room one evening and he was just staring at it in his hands. Mama, papa is in love with you, he can't marry Rebeca."

"Oh hush George, you don't know what you're talking about. Your papa cannot possib-"

"George? Who are you talking to?" Rebeca walked around the corner and scrunched her nose at who it was. "Annabel."

"Ms.Eckerman."

"I haven't seen you in a while. Honestly, I thought you'd run off and drown yourself with the way Richard screamed at you. Yes, he told me. But I see you work for the Wilton's now, a lovely family."

"Yes well,"

"Ms.Wilton," Rebeca interrupted Annabel. "Will I be seeing you at the party this Friday?"

"Yes, and Annabel as well."

George's eyes lit up. He wasn't going to go, but now he must. He'll tell Maggie so she could come as well.

"As your nan-"

"As my guest." Tiffany cut Rebeca off. She hooked her arms with Annabel. "I'll see you then George."

"Of course. Save a dance for me." He called out to her as they left the store.

"The first one!" She called over her shoulders.

"I see now why you said Rebeca wasn't a nice person." Tiffany spoke up. They lapsed into silence when her face quirked up to a mischievous grin.

"So Richard Pelton is in love with you." Tiffany teased Annabel as they walked down the street.

"He's not."

"Put he positively is."

"He is not."

"I'll double your salary if he comes knocking on our door this evening to "pay papa a visit" when he's really coming to see you the second George speaks up about bumping into you today and where you work."

"He won't, and you already randomly double my salary. Which I don't even know why you do."

"Because you tolerate my mothers and siblings bad mouth. Now, let's get you all prettied up for a certain Mr.Pelton. Not that I need to do much, you're already pretty."

"Even if he does come. I will not go to see him, no matter what you say."

The Party

"You wouldn't believe who we ran into today while shopping for a dress for the party this Friday." Rebeca twirled her fork in the air and gave Richard a you wouldn't believe it look.

George looked up at her, he wasn't expecting her to be the one bringing it up. Maggie looked at her older brother for further details, but he just smiled at her. It was rare for George to join them for dinner nowadays, even more rare to see him smile, so who ever it was, made him smile again.

"Pray tell, who?" Richard said with a slight annoyed tone to his voice, it was getting exceedingly hard for him to put up with Rebeca.

"You tell him George."

All eyes turned to George as he cleared his throat in surprise.

"We saw mama."

Maggie gasped, Richards hand froze from cutting the steak and his eyes opened wider, the twins happily looked at each other and hugged and Margot, well, she started calling out to her again.

"Y-you," Richard cleared his throat and tried again. "You saw Annabel?"

His heart was fluttering.

"Yes, she works for the Wilton's now, believe it or not." Rebeca put a forkful of food in her mouth.

"Old Wilton's gotten sick to the point of being bedridden and I haven't visited him in a while. I think it's about time I stoped by to see how he's doing , don't you think George?" Richard wiped his mouth and put the napkin down, getting up from his seat.

"I do, I'll even accompany you." George pushed his chair back and got up.

"Where do you two think you're going? It's lunch time, people are eating right now. You can't just barge in unannounced." Rebeca annoyingly sighed at them.

"James!" Richard called out and the butler hurriedly came into the dinning room. "Call the Wilton's and tell them that George and I will be stopping by this evening to check in on old man Wilton."

"Of course sir."

George sat back down and got kicked under the table by his sister.

"Why didn't you tell me?" She hissed at him.

"I was going to, but she beat me to it."

"So ah," Richard sat back down and shifted in his seat. "How is she doing?"

Maggie and George smirked at each other.

"How am I supposed to know? Get this, she's going to the party on Friday. In what? Her hand me downs?" Rebeca laughed out loud like what she said was the most hilarious thing in the world, but no one else laughed.

"You know papa, I know you told me a few days ago to come along to this party and I refused, but I think I've changed my mind now." Maggie gave her father a sweet smile.

He raised a brow at her but didn't say anything. He has a feeling he knows why she changed her mind.

Later that evening Tiffany was following around Annabel as she and her younger siblings picked their toys up to put away.

"He's going to come." She said for the millionth time that day.

"I'd much rather if he didn't." Annabel grumbled as she continued to work.

"Deep down you do."

They both stared at each other when the door bell rung.

"It's gotta be him!" Tiffany excitedly squealed and ran out of the room.

"It's most definitely not." Annabel huffed, but she was still curious and walked out of the room, down the hallway and peaked around the corner, down the stairs to the open door where the butler was greeting whoever it was.

"Thank you for having us on such short notice."

Her hand flew to her heart as it skipped a beat once she heard a voice she hasn't heard in a long time. She leaned back onto the wall and tried to calm her racing heart and slightly flushed cheeks. She was amazed and terrified of the strong effect his voice alone had on her.

Movement on the second floor caught Richards eye and he could swear it was a Annabel. He wanted, more than anything, to run up those stairs and find her. He needed to apologise to her. He needed her to come back home, for their kids, for him.

"Old man Wilton, he's upstairs in his room?" He strained his neck to see her and tried to move for the stairs.

"Actually sir, he managed to come downstairs into the living room to greet you." The butler motioned to the living rooms direction and Richard felt slight disappointment.

"I didn't think I'd be seeing you again so soon." Tiffany came down the stairs with a smile on her face as George grinned up at her.

"Ms. Wilton." He walked towards her and helped her down the last step.

"Where's mama?" He whispered to her.

"Upstairs. Nothing I say will bring her down." She whispered back, but then she turned to Richard. "A pleasure to have you in our house Mr.Pel ton."

"Ms.Tiffany, it's been a while." He tilted his head towards her.

"This way gentleman." She led them to the living room where her weak, frail father was sitting in his favourite seat.

"Wilton, my friend, it's been too long." Richard greeted his old friend and they sat and conversed like no time has even passed, but the entire time, Annabel was on Richards mind to the point that any noise coming from inside the house would get his heart racing and him sitting upright in case it was her and she was about to walk in.

George and Tiffany hit it off and in no time the two of them became close. They talked and brainstormed many ideas on how to get Annabel and Richard back on speaking terms and if possible, to actually get them together.

"This Friday?" Tiffany asked.

"This Friday." George confirmed.

*

On the day of the party things whizzed and happened so fast, Annabel didn't even realise what was happening until they were walking in the big ball room.

"Tiffany, I don't think this is a good idea." Annabel whispered and gripped Tiffany's arm in slight fear at the big, intimidating venue.

It was all bright with chandeliers, polished floors that were so bright she could see her reflection, a music band in the corner that has already started playing and the amount of incredibly rich people already present.

"I don't fit in."

"Yes you do. You look better than half the women here."

"What about the other half?"

Tiffany gave her a pointed look.

"Annabel, you're going to be fine. You'll fit right in, don't worry. Look, you've already caught a few mens attention, although it's not from anyone you should care about. Say, where's Richard?"

"He'll be here? Then it's definitely not a good idea for me to stay. That man hates me." It pained her more than she liked to admit when she said that. "I shouldn't be here Tiff."

"Yes you should. Live a little Annie. You have to make him jealous."

"Jealous of what?"

"Just jealous. Here's the plan-"

"There is no plan."

"George and I thought-"

"You got George into this!?"

"- up this amazing plan. It's fool proof, trust me. He'll see you dancing in the arms of another man, get jealous and whisk you away. He'll take you back and wife you up and then you two will have the most adorable children and I will be the best au-"

"Tiffany, that's enough. None of what you said is going to happen. Mr.Pe lton is engaged and soon to be married. It's not proper to say these things. Get these fantasies out of your head."

"But you would make the most wonderful chi-"

"I think it's time I head home." Annabel turned around and began heading the other way.

"Annabel! Come back, I'll stop, I promise." Tiffany went after her.

"No, we both know that-" Annabel suddenly turned around and walked to Tiffany. Both girls held onto each others arms.

"What? What is it?" Tiffany searched Annabel's spooked eyes.

"He's here. Richards here, what do I do?"

Tiffany looked behind Annabel and sure enough, Richard, his fiancé, and his two eldest kids were walking in. She then looked around her, grabbed the nearest man and shoved both him and Annabel to the dance floor.

"My friend here is a little shy. Why don't you show her the dance floor?" She gave the man a shut it look when he looked back at her in surprise and panic.

"Tiffany!" Annabel glared at her friend who just continued to push them until they were on the dance floor.

"I'm really sorry about her." Annabel apologised to the gentleman in front of her as they forcibly began to dance together to the music with the other dance couple.

"It's alright. I don't mind dancing with a beautiful lady like yourself." He smiled at her and she awkwardly laughed.

"Why thank you."

Richard scanned the crowd and his eyes fell on the most ethereal women he has ever laid eyes on. Her awkward smile, her beautiful brown hair, her glowing skin, the way her dress moved and how the colour complimented her so well. It set his soul on fire. Annabel set his soul on fire.

And it bothered him more than words can describe and more than he cared to admit that she was dancing in another man's arms.

Without even realising what he was doing, his feet moved on their own, away from his family and fiancée, to her.

"Annabel." He breathed out.

The song had just finished and she had just curtsied to the man in front of her while he bowed. The man looked up behind her at someone and she was about to turn, but froze when she heard her name coming from his lips.

Her dance partner gave her a quick smile and left, leaving her alone to deal with Richard.

"Would you turn around?" He asked softly, one of his hands going up and gently holding her elbow.

"Mr.Pelton, I don't think you should-"

He turned her around and they began dancing once the music came on, holding each other at a slight distance while they twirled and whirled to the slightly more upbeat song.

"Richard, I thought I told you to call me Richard when we're alone." He said when he pulled her closer in and then had to twirl her out again.

She looked even more beautiful and he didn't even know how that was possible.

"Well we're not alone, are we?"

He smiled at her cleverness, but then it dropped.

"I stopped by the Wilton's the other day when George told us that's where you work now. I was maybe hoping-"

"What? That I would come down and greet you? Why would I do that? You kicked me out, I do not owe you a greeting, or this dance actually. I would much rather go back to the Wilton's house and be getting ready for bed than be here."

"Then why come in the first place? You hate these events."

She couldn't tell him that he was the main reason she was there.

They continued to dance silently although it felt loud and suffocating, each was drowned in their own thoughts. People around the dance floor whispered amongst themselves about the mysterious women dancing with Mr.Pelton. Who is she to capture his attention the second he walks in the room that he makes a beeline for her and has his first dance of the evening with her and not his fiancée?

"Come home Annabel."

She ignored his pleading eyes and stared at a spot on his shoulder.

"How are the kids doing?"

"They'd be better if you were around."

"But I'm not. I wonder why?" She gave him a pointed look and he looked away.

"I'm sorry. I shouldn't have yelled that night. I shouldn't have overreacted. I shouldn't have let you go. Would you come home now? Our kids-the kids really need you Annie. Things are falling apart and-"

"Well it's nice to know you feel sorry for that night. But I can't just pack up and move back in. I have responsibilities to deal with at the Wilton's and children to look after. Plus, I'm sure the kids new nannie would do just fine. Now excuse me, I'm feeling a little thirsty."

The song ended and she moved away from him, but he followed her.

"They don't have a new nannie." He said as they weaved between the crowd.

"And why on earth is that?"

"Rebeca likes looking after them."

"I'm sure she does."

"That sounds very sarcastic."

"It is. Now please leave me alone. I have a friend to find and you have a fiancée to get to. It was very improper of you to have your first dance with me."

"Who cares about what's proper?"

She furiously turned around and jabbed a finger in his chest.

"You, I can't believe you! Your children's and your family's image does. Don't ruin it, and you will continue to ruin it if you keep following me and talking to me. Your fiancée is furiously marching over here, pull yourself together Richard."

She turned around and continued to the drinks table.

"Margot's sick."

She froze.

"What?"

"She has a high fever."

"And what exactly are you doing here?" She slowly turned around, clear annoyance and anger in her eyes.

"W-well I'm at a-"

"Are you being serious right now? Did you even leave a single maid to look after her?"

He shook his head no.

"I can't believe you. I actually can't believe you! You left your three year old daughter, unattended, and sick. I at least had others take turns to babysit them while I was out on a stroll, while you left her no one! Do you see how badly you're contradicting yourself right now Richard? This is the exact reason why you fired me. I honestly cannot believe you."

She slightly lifted the front of her dress and hurriedly made her way out of the party.

"I cannot believe him. That stupid, stupid man." She mumbled under her breath.

Richard ran after her, pushing past people.

"Papa, where are you going?" Maggie followed her slightly frantic father, George right behind her.

"Follow mama, we're going home." He said to her.

"You saw mama?"

"Didn't you see? He was even dancing with her." George said.

The siblings shared a look and grinned.

A Fever and Back With The Pelton's

Annabel got in a cab and told the man to go to the Pelton estate. Her knee was bouncing up and down in slight anxiety at what state she will find Margot in. She couldn't believe Richard would leave her and the twins alone without any sort of supervision, but it was also very unlike him to do something like that. He cared so much for his children, she wondered how the thought of leaving a sick baby alone even crossed his mind.

"Thank you." She paid the cab driver and rushed out.

"Welcome home sir, you've come back earlier than-Annabel?" James said as he opened the door.

"Good to see you too James. Now excuse me, I must get going."

"Papa?" Sam and Tam groggily rubbed their eyes, holding hands and walked up to the railing. Their eyes trailed down and instead of their papa, it was someone they weren't expecting.

"Mama!"

They rushed down the stairs and Annabel engulfed them in a hug.

"Oh Sam," she kissed his head, "Tam." she kissed hers.

"It's so good to see you two."

"Mama are you coming back? Are you staying forever?" Sam asked and pulled back to see her.

"Mama you're staying, right?" Tam pulled back and pulled Annabel's eye lid in wonder at the makeup. "Mama you look pretty."

She put both her small hands on Annabel's cheeks and turned her head so she was looking at her hair.

"Me too. Can you make my hair too?"

"I'd love to. I'll even play with the two of you, but first, we have to go see how Margot is doing. Don't you think?" She picked up Tam, wrinkling her dress, but she didn't care, and she held Sams hand as he led her to their shared room with their younger sister.

"Hey Mar Mar." Annabel put Tam down and made her way over to Margot's bed where she was laying down in nothing but diapers. Her body was sweating, a fresh coat of sweat was covering her entire body and the sheets she was on top of were drenched.

Her eyes were closed and her face was scrunched in pain as waves of heat rocked through her body that were then replaced by sudden chills and then intense heat again.

"Oh you poor thing."

Annabel picked up Margot and placed her on Tams bed.

"Tam, Sam. Mama needs help. You go get mama a bowl full of cold water. And you get mama a towel for Margot's forehead, okay?" She told the twins, they both nodded and ran out of the room.

She quickly changed Margot's sheets and pillow cover. She grabbed her a light blanket and draped it over her once she put her back in her bed.

Richard barged into the house and ran up the stairs, ignoring James who was calling after him and he made his way to the twins and Margot's room. The twins quickly ran past him, one with a bowl of sloshing water and another holding an entire stack of towels.

"We got you the things mama!" Tam dropped the towels at the foot of the bed and Sam gently placed the bowl on the night stand.

"Thank you, you're being very helpful." She kissed their foreheads, put a towel in the water, rung it out and placed it on Margot's forehead. She glanced over their heads to see Richards looking from the doorway.

"She's burning up." She spoke up and turned back to Margot, wiping her hair from off her face. Richard made his way into the room, grabbed a chair and sat across from Annabel. He studied her face, but then he looked at his daughters pained face and guilt washed over him. He hadn't realised just how sick she was. Rebeca said it wasn't that bad, when it clearly was.

"Will she be okay?" Tam tugged on her dress.

"I'm sure she will." She affectionately placed her hand on Tams cheek and rubbed it with her thumb. "Now, why don't you hop into your bed over there and get some rest, hmm? I'm sure you're tired."

"But I would like to help."

"But you've already helped me so much. If I need anymore help I'll make sure to tell you." She kissed her head and Tam kissed her cheek then climbed into her bed, Sam going into his.

When the children fell asleep, Richard spoke up.

"Will you stay?"

"Who's been looking after the kids?" She ignored his question.

He sighed and his head dropped between his elbows that were resting on his knees. Annabel realized, from his reaction, that no one has.

"I don't understand. You really care for them and love them. Why haven't you got anyone to look after them?"

"Rebeca's looking after them." He looked up to meet her eyes, but looked away from her calculating stare.

"And she's been doing a marvelous job I see."

"She's trying. She's new to all this mothering thing."

"Mr. Pelton I suggest you get your children a nanny or governess or whatever you want to call the job and have your fiancé learn a thing or two from her. Now, here's what's going to happen in the meantime and there's no negotiations. I love these kids, very much. And I can't stand the thought of one of them being sick without any proper care. So I will be staying until Margot gets better. You have until then to find them a new nanny."

"Will you call me Richard?" He slightly sat up. Something, relief, washed over him at knowing that she'll be back, even if it was for a little while.

"Really? That's what you get after all I just said, Mr.Pelton?"

"Richard."

"Mr.Pelton."

"Richard."

"If you continue to act childish your children will wake up."

They stared at each other, neither willing to back down.

She sighed and looked away while he slightly smirked.

"Fine, Richard. Anyways, I still have the Wilton children to take care of, so I'll stop by in the evenings, stay the night and go back in the morning. I expect Margot to be looked after while I'm gone."

He got up from his seat and looked down at her with a smile.

"I'll personally tend to Margot. Thank you for doing this Annabel."

She looked up at him and lightly blushed, but scrunched her eyebrows slightly together.

"I'm not doing this for you."

"I know, still th-"

"Are you two done being lovey dovey? I'd like to see mama now." Maggie crossed her arms at her father who gave her a sheepish smile as he walked out.

"We're not being lovey dovey." Annabel got up from her chair and hugged Maggie tight as she walked into the room.

"You might have denied it, but he hasn't. I don't know if you've realized it yet, but papa is head over heals for you."

"Why is this the first thing you say to me from not seeing each other for an entire month?"

"Because you two are stupid and in love."

"We are not."

"Totally are."

"Maggie."

"I give you my blessing by the way. I'd totally want you to be my real mama, not that you aren't, but you know."

"Maggie."

"What? I just wanted to let you know that you have it."

Winter Break And A Trip to Switzerland

"I can't."

"Yes you can." George sat in the arm chair as Annabel packed.

"George, I appreciate the invite, but no. I've already overstayed my welcome. Margot's been better for a while now, but I kept coming to check up, just in case."

"The younger ones think you'll be coming." He said in hopes she will change her mind.

"I've already told them I won't." She victoriously smirked at him while he groaned.

"You need a break. Take one this winter break and come with us to Switzerland." He frustratedly said and got up.

"I took a break. It was a week long, right after your father told me to leave." She put a dress inside her bag only for George to pull it out.

"That doesn't count. You were sick because of the rain for the entire weak."

"Who told you?"

"I heard you and Samantha talking."

"Well technically it is a break from working. Now Georgie fold that dress and put it back in the bag."

He groaned but did it anyways.

"Thank you. I'll be off."

She grabbed her scarf, wrapped it around her neck, took a hold of her bag and headed out her room and down the stairs.

"Leaving mama?" Margot walked up to her and held her bag to help carry it, although it was much too heavy.

"Unfortunately yes, but Maggie will bring you to visit, don't worry."

Margot nodded and focused really hard on slowly going down the stairs.

"Well, I'll see when you come back from Switzerland, if you don't forget about me." She winked at Maggie who was waiting down by the door and ruffled Sam's hair.

"Never!" The twins said at the same time.

"I'd hope not, see you then." She kissed all of their heads and they hugged and kissed her in return.

She walked outside and down the front steps.

This time, her leaving was a lot better than the time before. There was no pain, no tears, no rain, no screaming and shouting, and leaving things on a bad note. This was better.

Richard was waiting at the bottom of the front door stairs, leaning against his car. He watched as Annabel made her way down the stairs carefully, being mindful of the snow.

"Thank you for letting me stay and check up on Margot and the kids, but I'll be leaving now." She said and walked right past him.

"Umm Annabel."

She paused and glanced at him.

"Would you like a ride to the Wilton's?" He motioned to the car.

"I'm alright. I've been walking back and forth everyday. I also don't trust car tires in the snow, they're always slipping."

"Right, well, um, yeah, okay, be safe."

She found it amusing that he was slightly flustered.

"Thank you, you as well. Safe travels."

*

Tiffany and George hung up on the phone. They had just went over their plan and it was fool proof. It was bound to work.

"Father." She walked into her parents room where her father was sitting up on the bed and leaning against the head board. He had gotten better and was able to move around slightly.

"Ah, Tiffany. How have you been my daughter?" He lifted an arm as an invitation and Tiffany sat down beside him.

"I've been well. Thank you for asking. You're also looking better."

"I'm feeling better."

"That's good. It's great, really, so because you're feeling better and I'm also sure a change of scenery will make you feel even better. What do you-"

"You want us to go on a trip?"

"Yes! Precisely, wait how did you know?" She looked up at him with surprise while he chuckled.

"I may be getting slightly old, but I have still have very good hearing. You and that Pelton boy are planning something."

"If you must know," she shrugged and changed her position so she was sitting in front of him, but cross legged. "we are planning something."

He gave her a look to keep going.

"We're trying to sabotage Mr.Peltons engagement with Rebeca." She said happily while her father looked at her with horror.

"Tiffany!"

"Wait! I'm not done talking. We want Mr.Pelton and Annabel to get married instead. They are a much better match, don't you think?"

"I wouldn't know. I've been sick for a while."

"Exactly why we need to go to Switzerland next week with the Peltons. You're good friends with Mr.Pelton, aren't you? We could call it a big family trip. A bonding trip if you will. But father, you have to see Mr.Pelton and Annabel interact. It's so frustrating. They're clearly so in love with each other but neither one of them would like to admit it. We're just helping them. You'll see, Mr.Pelton doesn't even care about Ms.Von Eckerman. Whenever Annabel is around his attention is solely on her."

"I'm slightly concerned with how invested you are in this relationship."

"You would be too."

Mr.Wilton thought about it for a little while. He would like it if what his daughter said was true. He'd tease Richard all the time about it and he'd love to see his friend find love again.

"What do you say father?" Tiffany looked at her dad with pleading eyes and when he gave her the look that said yes she jumped up and cheered in happiness. "Yes! You won't regret it! I promise. You'll be wanting them to get together in no time!"

She kissed her fathers cheek and ran out the room to go call George and tell him the good news.

*

"I can't believe you got your father to agree to go on a trip to Switzerland." Annabel said as they were loading the cars to go to the airport. "With the Peltons."

"It wasn't even that hard." Tiffany had a smug look on her face.

"Sure, whatever you say." They shut the boot of the car and got in.

*

"It's good to see you up and walking again." Richard greeted Mr.Wilton with a hug when they finally meet up with them after getting their bags checked in and past security.

Mr.Wilton was about to reply but he noticed that something caught Richards attention over his shoulder and nothing he would have said would snap him out of his trance.

"Annabel..." He went around Mr.Wilton to her. "Let me."

He reached forward and plucked her bag out of her hand, ignoring her protest and turned around to face the rest of the group.

"Shall we, everyone?"

Rebeca gave Annabel a dirty glare, understandably so, and huffed on.

"What did I tell you?" Tiffany said as she walked past her father so she was next to George.

"Ugh since your hands are empty, you can carry this now, here." Amelia, Mrs.Wilton, said and gave Annabel her overly packed carry on bag.

"Yeah, sure, break my back while you're at it won't you?" Annabel said under her breath when she fell down slightly from the weight of the bag.

"Did you say something?"

"No ma'am." She gritted her teeth, stood straight, adjusted the bag and followed everyone while occasionally herding the Wilton children away from running into other people and from just running away.

*

"Will you be joining us for this evenings ice skating?" Richard asked Annabel from across the round dinning table they were seated at the hotel they were in.

"Mr. Pelton I think you keep forgetting that I am actually not on vacation, but still looking after Mr. and Mrs. Wilton's children." She coolely replied.

"Exactly, so you don't need to keep worrying yourself over her Mr. Pelton. I understand she used to work for you, but that was a long time ago." Amelia laughed like what she said was hilarious and Rebeca joined in.

"I'd argue that a nearly month and a half aren't that long of a time." George said.

"That's right, it only has been a month and a half of you being with us Annie. You must miss the Pelton children and Mr. Pelton very much." Tiffany said.

Annabel looked up at Richard then her eyes went back down to her plate.

"Yes, I do miss the Pelton children, but I've been seeing them recently and we're all here on the same trip together, aren't we?" She gave Maggie, George, the twins, and Margot a warm smile that they all returned.

"And we've also missed you mam-" A look from Annabel got Maggie to change what she was saying mid sentence, "Ms.Annabel. It's really different when you're not around."

Richard looked up at his daughter with confusion written across his face.

"Ms. Annabel? Ahh, since when did you call her that?"

Maggie looked at Annabel for help and she spoke up.

"I asked the children to stop calling me by the other name."

"I'm-I'm confused. Why would you do that?" He looked slightly hurt that she would ask them to stop calling her mama.

"Well, I'm sure it makes Ms.Von Eckerman extremely uncomfortable seeing that she is about to become their stepmother. And I don't work for you anymore, so they shouldn't be calling me that."

"Thank you for finally understanding. Yes, it made me extremely uncomfortable." Rebeca said with a too large of a smile on her face. Annabel gave her a smile in return and avoided Richards gaze that was penetrating through her.

"Umm, Ms. Annabel." Thomas, Mr.Wilton's eleven year old, tuged on her dress. She turned in her seat and looked at him.

"Do you need help with anything Thomas?"

"I'm done eating. What do I do now?"

"Oh, well, I'm also done and it looks like Oliver and Grace are also finished, so we could go back up to the rooms and get some sleep. How does that sound?"

Mr. Wilton also had five children, the oldest being Tiffany who was twenty three, then it was James at 20, Oliver was 14, Grace just turned 13 and the youngest, Thomas, he was eleven.

"Okay." He nodded and got up from his chair.

"Where are you heading off to Tom?" Mr. Wilton asked.

"I'm going to bed, good evening everyone."

Oliver and Grace followed their younger brothers lead and also got up.

"Us too."

"Can we go to bed?" The twins asked and without an answer, they got up and dashed to Annabel's side, each holding one of her hands.

"Me!" Margot hopped off her chair, stumbled and then got up and ran to Annabel, she held on to Tams hand.

"Since Grace is going to bed, then I should too." Maggie got up and that left all the adults sitting at the table.

"Don't worry Ms.Von Eckerman, I'll take them all to bed so you just enjoy yourself while out skating." Annabel said and took all the children with her back up to their rooms.

*

"I don't understand. Why can't we go skating with the adults? George, James and Tiffany are all going." Grace whined and fell back on the bed.

"That's because they're adults." Annabel said, walking in with Margot balanced on her hip.

"When will we become adults!" She huffed and turned to Maggie who was laying down on the other side of the bed. "When we're adults, we'll go skating as many times as we want."

"Then we'll get bored." Maggie replied.

Sam and Tam came crying, running away from Thomas and Oliver who had sheets over their heads and were pretending to be ghosts.

"Here you go." Annabel handed them each a pillow and they used it to beat the two boys up.

"Annabel have you ever gone skating before?" Grace sat up, a pillow in her lap.

"No I haven't."

"Oh, I didn't think so. Anyways Maggie, what do you say we go up on the big hill tomorrow?"

"I don't mind, but can you ski properly?"

"I can, can you?"

"Of course I can."

Annabel let the two girls be and went out into the living room to check on the two boys and the twins.

Mr.Wilton and Mr.Pelton both reserved the entire floor which was divided into two. Richard reserved one half and Mr.Welton the other. So, it was large and fit everyone, the doors between the two were always open seeing that they were the only rooms on the floor. Both suites consisted of living rooms, a bar, and more than enough bedrooms. The children decided to sleep over in Grace and Oliver's rooms. The two rooms also happened to be adjacent to each other, a door connecting the two, so it too was open and they were running back and forth between the rooms.

"If you keep jumping on the couch Thomas, you will hurt yourself."

Just as she said that, Thomas fell off from the couch.

"I told you. Time for bed everyone, let's go."

Thomas stuck his tongue out at her and ran to his room.

"Hey! That was awfully rude!" Sam shouted at him and then ran after him on his much shorter legs.

Annabel sighed and took Tams hand and led her to the girls room ; she was going to sleep with Grace and Maggie. She tucked the girls in and then went to the boys room where Sam, Oliver and Thomas were sleeping.

"Don't be too loud now." Annabel told them, and turned off the lights. "Come on, I guess you'll be sharing with me tonight." She said to Margot and they headed to her room.

"I'm not sleepy." Margot said, rubbing her eyes and yawning.

"I could read you a story?"

"Okay."

*

"You seem awfully fond of Ms.Annabel." Mr.Wilton casually said when Richard stepped off the ice to warm up by the fire.

"Where's this coming from?" Richard avoided direct eye contact.

"It's just an observation."

"I'm not. She's just a good governess or whatever for my children." He mumbled and quickly went back on the ice.

"Oh? You're definitely in love my good friend." Mr.Wilton smirked.

Frostbites

The hotel on the ski mountain the Wilton's and Pelton's were staying at, held an annual snowman building competition for all ages. Lots of people stopped by and many participated, seeing that it was a fun family and individual activity to partake in.

"I'm going to make a snowman so big you won't even see the sky!" Oliver said as he pulled on his gloves.

"Mine will be bigger than yours." Thomas said, pulling on his boot.

"We'll see. Loser does whatever the winner asks for an entire day. Deal?" Oliver held his hand out and Thomas shook it.

"Deal."

"Hey, have you seen where my fluffy socks are?" Grace walked into Annabel's open room. She was pulling a toque on.

"Should be stuffed to the side in your suit case."

"Okay, if I can't find it can I borrow one of yours?"

"Maggie's will fit better."

"Good point." And she walked out to ask Maggie to borrow a pair of her fluffy socks instead of looking for her own.

"So you're right." Mr.Wilton said to Tiffany while they sat on the couch in the living room.

"I'm always right, but what is it for this time?" She asked.

"Richard and Annabel, it's clear as day."

"Yes! I knew you would see it. So, will you help us?"

"You and George? I'll try my best. I too don't like Ms.Von Eckerman too much and think Annabel would be a better choice."

"I could always count on you, father." Tiffany kissed his cheek, got up and ran to Mr.Pelton's side of the floor to tell George the good news.

"We're leaving in five! The competition is about to begin!" Richard called out to everyone and they hurried to the elevator to take them down to the bottom floor. They had to do it in two go's because of how many they were so which ever family gets to the elevator first goes down and the second one has to wait.

The children were the first to the elevator and beat everyone down, so when it came back up, the adults all squeezed in.

Mr.Wilton bumped Annabel so she was standing next to Richard. One side of her was pressed against the elevator wall and the other was against Richard. Mr.Welton smirked and stood on the other side of Mr.Pelton, slightly stepping in his personal space so he shifted even closer to Annabel.

"Sorry, excuse me." Richard said under his breath as he was pushed against Annabel even more. He had to lift a hand and rest it on the wall beside them so he wasn't pressed against her too much and his shoulder wasn't uncomfortable, but that just made things even worse. His shoulder was a lot more comfortable, but now she was standing right underneath him. Her intoxicating smell wafted up his nose and he couldn't help but take another breath of it.

He heard his friend Austin Wilton snicker from beside him and he turned his head to give him a look only to find that he was victoriously smirking at him.

*

It was a day full of fun and laughter for everyone as they all built their snowmen, threw snowballs at each other and drank hot chocolate.

"Grace! This is for you!" Annabel called out and Grace ran over to her.

"What do I need a carrot for?" She took the long carrot in her hands and examined it.

"For the snowman's nose of course."

"Oh yes! I forgot about that!" She ran back to her snowman and stuck the carrot into its face.

"You don't happen to have an extra carrot nose do you?" Richard approached her.

"I ugh, I actually do. It's just small." She pulled out the carrot from her pocket and handed it to him.

"Thank you. Which ones yours?" Richard didn't want to leave just yet, he wanted to keep on conversing with her.

"That one over there. Tam, Margot and I are working on it together."

"And Sam?"

"He's found a new group of friends and they're building a very big one together, just over there. And look, over there is James, Tiffany and George. There's is quit good."

"It is, how about mine and Rebecca's, what do you think of it?"

"Which one is it?"

"Oh, I thought you would have known seeing that you know where every-one's snowmen are." He grinned at her and she smiled back.

"Only the childrens. I'm keeping track of them, I don't need to keep track of the adults."

"Right. That one over there."

She looked to where he was pointing and saw Rebecca try to carry the middle part of the snowman onto the bottom part and when she placed it on top, it cracked and both balls crumbled.

"Well, it needs some work that's for sure. But I'm sure it will look great once you're done with it." She patted his chest and went back to help the girls with their snowman.

Richard rubbed where she just patted him and grinned. When he went back to Rebecca she asked him why he was all smiley.

"I got us a carrot for his nose." He held up the carrot and he showed her, but his eyes trailed back to Annabel and Rebecca saw that and understood the real reason to his sudden happiness. Annabel probably gave it to him.

To say Rebecca was bothered by Annabel was an understatement. She was full on jealous of her. She didn't understand how her fiancé could ever look at someone of such lowly class like Annabel's. She couldn't see what he saw in her and she was beyond confused how he didn't pay much attention to her like he did to Annabel. She was far better looking and had a better upbringing and her family was deeply rooted in the society. She had ties and connections, while Annabel had none of that. Yet, when ever she walks in a room Richard gets captivated by her. Whenever she laughs, Richard smiles. Whenever she's taking care of the children in front of them, he's looking at her with the most loving gaze a women dreams of receiving. When he fired her, it was clear that she was the only person on his mind. Rebecca couldn't understand how someone who didn't have anything, still had more than her.

*

Margot suddenly began crying hysterically.

Richard sprang up from rolling the snowman's head and ran to his daughter which was already in Annabel's arms.

"Hey, you're okay. It's okay. Can you tell me what's wrong? Are you hurt? Where does it hurt Mar Mar?" Annabel pulled Margot's head down to her chest and placed a hand on top of her head for comfort as the girl continued to cry.

"Hey. What happened? Is she okay?" Richard fell down to his knees next to Annabel and put a hand on Margot's back in comfort. Panic coursed through him at the thought that something might be wrong or hurting his daughter.

Margot continued to cry but she held up her hands for her father to see. He quickly took off his and her gloves and held her hands.

"Oh God. They're freezing." He inclosed his hands around hers and tried to warm her up.

"She'll get even worse frostbites if she stays out here. I'll take her inside." Annabel began to stand up and Richard stood up with her.

"I'm coming."

"What seems to be the problem?" Rebeca walked up to them.

"She has frostbites." Richard said. He bent down and picked up the gloves.

"Oh poor thing. Here, let me take her. I know just how to make her feel better." Rebeca held her hands out and Annabel hesitantly handed her Margot. Richard was about to say something about how Annabel should help Morgan but he bit his tongue.

"It will be okay Morgan." Rebeca held the crying girl and made her way inside with Richard.

"Her names Margot!" Annabel called after her.

"Will she be okay?" Tam tugged on Annabel's snow coat.

"I hope so."

Frostbites (p2)

A nnabel couldn't even sit still anymore. Margot crying was what's been on her mind and she couldn't stop worrying.

"Tiffany!" She called out to the girl putting a scarf on her brothers, hers, and George's snowman. Tiffany turned to her and came running over.

"Please look after them for a while. I have to go back inside."

"Okay, take your time." Tiffany said and helped Tam put the three coal pieces on the snowman.

Annabel rushed back inside the hotel and was greeted by Margot crying in the foyer. Rebeca was clearly getting more frustrated with the girl and Richard was just getting more stressed. As if he sensed her, Richard spun around and faced Annabel. He quickly rushed to her.

"Nothing Rebeca is doing is working. What do we do?" He was panicked and freaking out.

Annabel rushed to Rebeca who was getting even more frustrated with Margot.

"Here, you take her. Nothing I'm doing is working." She angrily huffed and handed Margot to Annabel.

"What have you tried?" Annabel said and bounced Margot on her hips.

"Candy, hot chocolate, toys, it's just not working."

Annabel sighed in annoyance and rushed to the elevator.

"Because that's not how you treat frostbites." She said over her shoulders, Richard rushing after her.

"It's okay. I got you." Annabel said when they reached their floor and placed Margot on the couch on Mr.Peltons side. She immediately began taking Margot's wet, and freezing cold clothes off and threw them in a pile. Richard brought a towel and clothes.

"Warm water in the tub, please." She told him as she wrapped Margot in the towel. He rushed to the washroom to get the tub ready.

"See, your cold clothes are off. All you need is a nice soak in the warm tub." She picked her up and made her way over to where she heard running water.

"That's a little too hot, add cold water." She said when she tested the rising water in the tub. Richard switched the taps and added cold water. Annabel mixed the water around with her arm and when it was just right she told Richard to turn it off. She unwrapped Margot and placed her gently down in the tub. It wasn't fully filled, only up to Margot's shoulders when she's sitting down. This way, she wouldn't drown.

She immediately stopped crying and just sat sniffling in the tub.

"Does that feel a lot better?" Annabel said, sighing in relief. Margot nodded. Her fingers and toes were still way too cold and frozen to move around, but the warm water was definitely helping.

Richard sat on the floor, knees up and head between his shoulders as all the stress and worry left him. Annabel held his hand in comfort and gave his a reassuring squeeze.

Richard looked at their hands and pulled her down in between his legs.

"R-Richard?"

He turned her around so her back was pressed against his front and he wrapped his arms around her, pulling her closer and resting his chin on her shoulder.

"I just really need a hug right now." He mumbled and wrapped his arms tighter around her.

Annabel bit her tongue and instead of pushing him away like her brain told her to do, she did what her heart told her.

She shifted away from him and he thought she was pulling away.

"Please Annabel. I just, I really need you right now." He looked at her with pleading eyes. All she did was softly smile, turn around so she was facing him and wrap him up in a tight hug.

He was surprised to say the least, he never thought that she would ever hug him. He hesitantly wrapped his arms around her in case this wasn't real, but it was, and when he was sure of it, he held her tight and dug his nose in the crook of her neck.

"Are you feeling better now?" Annabel softly asked after a while of them just sitting on the ground and quietly holding each other in a warm, tight, safe embrace.

"Much."

She pulled away from the comfort and heat his body offered and looked up at his face.

"You're surprisingly quite nice to hug." She smiled at him and her cheeks turned slightly pink at the embarrassment of what she said.

"I like hugging you too." His soft smile reached his eyes and he brought a hand up to brush some stray strands of hair out of her face. His thumb then brushed her slightly flushed cheek and he held the side of her face with his hand.

"Annabel..." he studied her face and his eyes lingered on her lips more than once. "Come back home now."

His other hand snaked around her waist and pulled her closer as he slightly leaned more down.

"Come back home to the children. To me. They need you."

Their faces inched closer towards each other and she too studied his face, one arm was hung loosely around his neck while the other one played with the collar of his shirt.

"Just them?" She whispered, her eyes going up from staring at the collar, to his eyes and he was barely able to hear it. His heart beat faster and he was about to close the distance between them when Margot slightly slipped inside the tub and caused a splash. They snapped out of whatever was drawing them closer together and they quickly pulled away.

"Are you alright dear?" Annabel got up and peered down onto Margot who was regaining her balance. "How are your hands and legs?"

"Still cold." The three year old held her hands up for inspection and Annabel held them.

"Hmm, just a little longer and they'll be alright." She leaned down and kissed the tips of Margot's fingers before letting go of them.

Richard got up, feeling slightly dejected and headed to the door.

"Richard."

He stopped and looked back at her.

"How's your leg?"

They both glanced down at his leg that used to be injured.

"It's fine. Why do you ask?"

"It's just...your limps gotten worse ever since we got here."

His heart fluttered at her noticing him. He also didn't think anyone would take notice of his leg being worse.

"The cold bothers my leg and the strain of travel and activities has made it worse."

"Does it hurt?"

"Sometimes."

"Hmm." A thoughtful look crossed her face and seeing that she was too preoccupied with whatever is going on in her mind, Richard left the wash-room.

*

"Well, Mar's all better now. I changed her into her night wear and tucked her in." Annabel said as she walked into the living room. Margot's snow suit and towel in hand. She walked over to one of the chairs in the corner of the room beside the phone connecting to the foyer and hung the towel. She then hung the snow suit behind the door.

"She really had me worried there. I don't think I've ever been that worried bef-actually, I have." Richard said from his seat on the couch. He had his neck craned all the way back on the head rest and his eyes closed. He opened them and watched Annabel upside down as she picked up some of the kids toys lying around. She paused and urged him to continue with the look she gave him.

"Well..?"

"When you fell in that stream. I don't think I've ever ran that fast all my life." He grinned at her and she smiled back.

"I honestly thought I wouldn't make it."

"Have you learned to swim since then?"

"In the freezing winter? Yes, yes I have." She sarcastically said. She finished putting the toys away and sat on one of the couches, feeling slightly exhausted.

"Looks like I have to teach you come summer again."

"No thank you. I'd rather stay away from large bodies of water like that again."

"What if one of the kids falls in again? What then?" He curiously asked her and properly sat up.

"Well, I wouldn't be alone. I'd take you or George with me. Even Phil, the horse handler."

"No need to take Phil, I'll just go whenever you plan on going on a picnic near the stream." He sounded slightly agitated but she let it slide.

She studied his face while he stared down at his hands and came to the conclusion that they really need to talk.

"Richard."

"Annabel."

They both said at the same time. They both looked at each other before looking away.

"You first." She offered.

"No you."

She suddenly didn't know where to start and had a hard time sorting through her thoughts. Richard saw her internal struggle, he sat at the edge of the couch so he was closer to where she was sitting and reached for her hand. He ran his thumb over the back of her hand and looked up at her while she looked down at their hands.

"We can't...this, whatever this is. It has to stop." She took her hand away from his and instead held her own hand.

"What do you mean?" He knew exactly what she meant.

"You know what I mean. Hand holding, hugging, being so close to each other, it's not right. We have to stop." She looked into his eyes to get her point across.

"Why? What's so wrong about being friendly towards each other?"

"You know this is far more than just being friendly. You shouldn't be," she sighed and rung her fingers together, "you shouldn't be this close to another women when you're going to get married soon. It's not right, people will interpret it wrong, and your fiancée won't be happy with you."

He reached for her hand again and when she tried to pull away he held on tight.

"Why? Does it feel wrong to you?"

She looked away from him as he sat even closer.

"This?" He lifted their hands and intertwined them, "this doesn't feel wrong to me."

He brought their intertwined hands to his lips and kissed her fingers.

"Richard..."

"It feels so right Annabel. Tell me it feels right to you too. This," he brought his other hand and held their intertwined hands in it, "it makes me rethink everything."

"Stop."

"Why? Is it-"

"Enough Richard. You're going to be a married man soon. What ever this is. Whatever is going on in your head, forget about it." She pulled her hand away and got up. She wiped her hands on the sides of her pants in nervousness and made her way out of the room.

"Will you?" He called out.

She stopped and turned to look back at him.

"Will I what?"

"Will you also forget?"

She stayed silent and looked down at the ground.

"Is this why you won't come back home?"

She looked away and bit her bottom lips.

"I don't, I don't have a home here."

"Yes you do." He got up and took a few steps closer to her. "You have one. Up on that meadow in our town lies a house. It's your home, with me and the children."

"Home isn't defined by four walls. Home can be a person and my home is my mama. Who lives far away from me. But that doesn't matter, what matters is that house you're speaking about, it's stopped being my home the second you kicked me out." She looked at him and bit back the tears in her eyes.

"I didn't mean what I said back there. I apologise. I really do. If I could turn back the time, I would, and I would make it so I never said those words, ever."

"Well, you did." She turned away and went over to Mr.Wilton's side of the floor.

"No wait, Annabel." He rushed after her, but the elevator opening stoped him in the middle of his tracks. Rebeca walked out with Austin's wife.

"Annabel? Well, whatever. How is Margot?" She asked, her tone didn't seem like she cared, at all.

"Sleeping." He mumbled and limped back to their rooms.

"I'm telling you Beca, something is up with that fiancé of yours and that wretched nanny." Amelia said and Rebeca nodded.

"I have a feeling something might be up. Why don't you just fire her? It would ease my mind a whole lot."

The two friends walked into the Pelton's living room and sat down on the couches.

"I'll bring it up to Austin. He won't say no to me."

"Oh you must be very sad that his health is getting better." Rebeca said and held her friends hands in comfort.

"You have no idea. I was really looking forward to him passing away. I would have gotten part of the money he would be leaving behind."

"Let's look at the brighter picture shall we? As long as he's alive, more money comes in and the more you can spend." Rebeca said and they both laughed like witches.

Campfire Memories

"Something is terribly wrong." Tiffany barged into her fathers room.

"Don't startle me like that! What is it?" He jumped up from putting on his socks and held his heart.

"Annabel and Mr.Pelton."

"There's always something wrong with these two." He said and continued to wear his fuzzy socks.

"No, you don't get it. They won't even talk to each other anymore. They're not even looking at each other." She grabbed her fathers boots from beside the door and handed them to him.

"Thank you dear, and I guess that is a big problem. What do you think happened?"

"If I knew, I'd tell you. George is also trying to find out. We think it has something to do with when they brought Margot up here. When she had frostbites yesterday."

"Well, why don't you come up with a plan to get them talking to each other again?"

"We're also trying to do that. We're even getting Maggie's help. Say, what do you think, tonight, when we're all around the campfire and sharing stories and memories, we bring one up of them and see their reaction?"

"Wonderful idea. We can even get a little game of truth or dare going."

"Excellent! Father you're brilliant!" She kissed her fathers cheek and ran out of the room to tell George and Maggie.

*

"Pst, mama." Sam whispered to Annabel.

"Sam, what did we say? You can't call me that anymore." She scolded.

They were all seated on logs, in a circle around a camp fire. They had found sticks and George and James sharpened their ends with knives so they could put marshmallows on the ends of them and they were all currently roasting theirs.

"I know, but look at my marshmallow. It's on fire!"

Annabel quickly dropped her marshmallow in the snow and took Sam's stick and pulled it close to her.

"Oh God!" Rebeca screeched when she saw the fire increase on the marshmallow. Everyone turned to look.

Annabel quickly put out the fire and the smell of burnt marshmallow wafted up her nose.

"I'll get you another one." She got up, threw the marshmallow away and put a new one before sitting back down and handing it to him. "Be careful this time, and keep your eyes on it, alright?"

Sam nodded.

She looked down and noticed that her own marshmallow was also ruined, since she dropped it in the snow. She sighed and picked it up. She was about to get up and replace it with one of the marshmallows they had in the bag on the table when a stick got handed to her.

"You can have this one." Richard had gotten up from his seat across from her and handed her his. Without even waiting for her to respond, he took hers, switched it for a better one and sat back down in his spot.

She looked at the stick in bewilderment, then she just went along with it. She didn't even thank him or glance up at him.

George nudged Tiffany at the interaction between the two and she nodded, silently telling him that she noticed. Her father gave her a look from across the campfire and she grinned at him. This was some sort of progress.

"I think it's time to start the first plan." George whispered to her.

"I think so too."

Their first plan was to get Richard to hand out some s'mores. That way, him and Annabel will slowly start to interact before playing a big game like truth or dare.

She got up and headed to the table where they had extra packs of marsh-mallows lying around, a lot of graham crackers and chocolate spread. She spread chocolate on a lot of the graham crackers and laid them out so it's faster to get the s'mores done.

"If your marshmallow's done, bring it up here so I could do it for you." She called out and nearly everyone handed her their sticks. She called out their names to get their s'more and when it was Mr.Pelton's turn, she handed him two.

"That one's for Annabel. Would you please hand it to her? I'll be done quicker this way." She told him and quickly turned around to show him that the conversation is over. Richard stared at her for a few seconds, swearing that she was doing this on purpose, and then headed to Annabel.

"Here you go." He was staring straight ahead but he handed her the s'more.

"What's this?"

"A s'more."

"I can see that. Why are you handing it to me?"

"Tiffany said this one was yours."

"No thank you. I can get one myself." She got up to head to Tiffany when he stopped her.

"Just take it. There's nothing wrong with handing someone else a s'more. Or is there?" He glared at her and she glared right back.

"Give it to Rebeca."

"No, it's yours." He hissed at her and tried shoving it in her hands but she wasn't taking it.

"□□□□ I'll be taking my s'mores." She snatched both if the s'mores out of his hands and gave him a challenging stare.

"Hand that one back."

"No, it's mine. You gave it to me first."

"I only gave you one."

"And I took two. Do you have a problem?"

"Yes, I do. Now give it back."

"Fine, I never wanted them anyways." She shoved them back into his hands and turned around and started walking away.

"Where are you going?"

"To sleep."

"Annabel, come back here."

"No."

He growled in frustration, marched after her, dragged her back to the log and shoved her so she was sitting on it.

"Just take both of them. I can make more." He handed her the s'mores.

She stood up and they glared at each other.

"I don't want them. I'm not hungry anymore."

"Oh so you're hungry?"

"I'm not."

"You just said you are."

"I said I'm not anymore. Are you too dumb to understand?"

"You're going to eat them."

"I'm not." She handed them back to him.

"Yes you are." He handed them back.

Everyone was watching them go back and forth like it was a tennis match.

"No, I will not be eating them." She shoved them back in his hands.

"If you don't eat them this instance I will shove them down your throat."

"I dare you."

He took that as a challenge and attacked her with the s'mores. She screeched and tried to get away but he caught her and they fell on top of each other, rolling in the snow. Richard tried shoving the s'more into her mouth but she clamped it shut, so instead, it's was smudging all over her face.

"You will eat this." He shouted at her.

"I will not!" She shouted back and shoved his hands away. She took the other s'more out of his hand and flipped them over so she was straddling his front and had him pinned down. She shoved the s'more and smudged it all over his face.

"How does that feel Richard? Eat it all up won't you?"

He tried flipping her over so he was on top but she got away and started running to the hotel.

"You get back here this instance Annabel!" He shouted at her and balled up a snowball in his hand.

"Make me Pelton!" She screamed back and was hit square in the back of the head by the snowball and she fell face first into the snow. "I hate you! You're such a tosser!"

"And you're a daft cow!"

She got up from the snow, fuming. She marched back over and shoved her hand on his chest, making him stumble back.

"You take that back this instance."

"You take back what you said first."

"Never."

"Then I won't either."

"Sam, why are mama and papa fighting?" Tam whispered to her twin, but the two fuming adults heard and snapped their heads towards them.

"She's not your mama." Richard growled out.

"What he said." Annabel said.

"Oh look at you, agreeing to something I said." Richard turned to her with a mocking look on his face.

"Don't let that boost your ego. This is the only time this will ever be happening." She growled out at him.

"Enough! You two are acting like children!" Rebeca screamed out.

"Stay out of it!" Both Richard and Annabel both said, pointing at her, with very angry looks.

"Oh look, you agreed again."

"No I did not. We just happened to have said the same thing at the same time." She said.

"You totally did."

"I did no-you know what? That's it, I've had enough of you. I cannot stand you anymore. I can't continue this trip while you're here. I'm going back home."

"Home?" He said, all the energy from the fight went away and it felt like he was slapped in the face with a cold cloth at hearing that she can't stand him. But then slight hope at hearing the word home. Maybe she meant their home up in the meadow, but that hope was quickly put out when she spoke again.

"Yes, home. Back to my mother who I haven't seen in a long time. I'm leaving and I'll never see you again."

"If you leave, then you're fired." Mr. Wilton's wife spoke up.

"Then so be it. I quit. Good bye everybody." She spun around and headed inside the hotel.

Tiffany and George looked at each other in panic, as funny as this was, this was not supposed to happen. Everything happened so fast that no one knew how to react.

Richard stood there in utter shock, his heart breaking with every step she took away from him.

This was his fault. It was all his fault. He had to fix this. But would she come back? This is the second time he drives her away. He can't loose her again. But what if she really hated him now?

"Go papa! Go bring her back. Don't loose the women you love all over again!" George shoved his dad forward and Richard snapped out of it.

"The woman he loves?" Rebeca asked.

"Oh fuck off. Everybody knew he loved her and not you. Even you did." George said to her and grinned when he saw his father run after Annabel.

*

The elevator was taking too long for Richards liking so he rushed up the stairs, taking them two at a time even though it hurt his leg and he knew he was going to be in a lot of pain later.

He burst out of the stairwell and rushed to Mr.Wilton's side of the floor. He heard running water and followed it to the washroom where Annabel was vigorously rubbing her face clean of snow, s'mores and what seemed to be tears.

He walked up to her and whirled around when she heard him.

"Ri-"

He grabbed her face with both of his hands and smashed their lips together in a desperate kiss. He tried showing her, with that single kiss, just how much he wanted her to stay, just how much he needed her and how he couldn't let her go. How she's been driving him crazy and insane.

They would have continued their heated and desperate kiss if the need for air wasn't nagging them to pull apart.

They rested their foreheads against each other and tried catching their breaths. They both searched each other's faces and for once, found the answers to their unspoken questions.

"Your face is covered in s'mores." Annabel tried to hold in her laughter. He smiled wide and his eyes shone with happiness.

"Yours is too."

Home

"We're home!" Maggie called out as they walked into the large house. "And guess who's with us!"

Samantha rushed out of the kitchen and to the foyer. Her eyes light up when she saw Annabel helping with carrying some of the cases in.

"Annabel!" She called out to her. Annabel turned around and the two women hugged. "Are you back for good?"

"I don't know if it's for good," she looked back at the children with a smile on her face, "but, I am their nanny again."

"Oh that's just wonderful news!" Samantha crushed her in a hug again.

"Welcome home Miss. Annabel." The butler said as he walked past her. He played it cool, but he was very glad she was back. He was starting to miss her laughter and crazy antics.

"Thank you." She said back to him.

Samantha caught the longing look Richard gave Annabel when he walked in and she gasped.

"What's wrong?" Annabel asked her.

"Did you...are you and Sir. Oh God, I'm so happy! You have to tell me what happened." She excitedly said and clutched Annabel's hands.

"Nothing happened." Annabelle's reassured her. "Actually, something did. Something big, but that's up to Mr.Pelton to tell you."

Just then Samantha noticed that Rebeca wasn't with them.

"Pray tell, where is that talking trash bag?" She said in a quiet voice.

Annabel only smiled at her.

"Up to Mr.Pelton."

*

It was over dinner time that Richard Pelton dropped the bomb on everyone. Granted, he already told Annabel days before.

"I'd just like to announce that my engagement to Rebeca Von Eckerman has been called off. We will not be seeing each other anymore." He randomly said at one of the very few quiet intervals.

The children all stopped eating, Maggie's mouth hung open with unchewed food, George spat out the juice he was drinking, the twins just stared at their father and Margot continued to eat.

"I don't like Eckerman. Happy I don't see her again." Margot said and gave her dad a thumbs up.

Excited chatter filled the dinning room, Richard couldn't remember when was the last time he saw his kids brim with so much happiness and energy.

"Did they really hater her that much?" He asked Annabel as she walked behind him and to the other side of the table to help Sam with cutting his food.

"Oh yes, I'm surprised you haven't noticed until now."

He just shook his head at his own oblivion, but he had a smile on his face. He might have noticed it late, but at least Rebecca wasn't here anymore and Annabel was. The women he truly loved, not that she knew that.

After Annabel was sure the younger kids could handle themselves, she too sat down and began eating her dinner.

Everyone conversed in light conversation and laughter was heard throughout the entire house, something that wasn't heard when Rebeca was around.

Dessert came, vanilla ice cream with a side of warmed up brownie and chocolate sauce.

"So, I've been wondering." Maggi said, dipping her spoon in the ice cream. She looked up at her father and then at Annabel. "Have you two kissed yet?"

Annabel choked on her food and began coughing. Richard immediately got up from his chair and went over to her, handing her his glass of water and patting her back.

"Thank you," Annabel said once she stopped coughing.

"So you have? Just from that reaction alone-"

"Maggie." Richard gave his daughter a warning glare.

"But I was just wondering if-"

"I don't know why you would ever think that, but no, we haven't. Satisfied?" Annabel also gave her a look to drop the subject.

"Fine, okay. I won't ask anymore. But if you do kiss, I have to be the first one to know."

"Maggie!" They both said at the same time.

*

"Do you love papa?" Tam asked in her sweet innocent voice while Annabel tucked them in for bed.

"Well, love is a pretty strong word don't you think?" Annabel said, bringing the comforter up to Sams chin and kissing his forehead.

"I don't know. I think it's a nice word. I mean, I love you. And I love Sam and Margot. Even Maggie, but sometimes she's annoying. I also love Papa and George and Samantha. I love a lot of people. Sometimes, I feel like the word love isn't enough for how much I actually love someone. It's not big enough."

Annabel went to Tams bed and sat on the edge of it.

"That's a lot of love you got there Tam."

"Is that a bad thing?"

Annabel smiled and brushed hair away from the girls face.

"No, I don't think so. I also love many people."

"Like, how many?"

"So much I need more than my fingers to count them all."

"Like this much?" Tam held up her hands and pulled Annabel's hands up too.

"I think so."

"That's a big number."

"It is, but it's such a lovely feeling to love somebody and to have them love you back. I think it's a blessing to be able to love and be loved."

"Like you and papa? You two love each other, right?

"I-"

"His eyes get all big and sparkly when you walk in the room. They really do," she sat up and opened her eyes wide to show Annabel what she meant, "and then Maggie says that when he's staring into nothing and is smiling all silly, that's because he's thinking about you. And Samantha told me, if you really love someone, then you run after them when you fight, and didn't papa run after you? He did, didn't he? And then remember the time he carried you home after you fell in the river, and he stayed by your side all night because you got a little sick? And you looked after him when he hurt his leg, and you make sure he gets out of the office and spends time with all of us when he stays in there for soooo many hours. And your cheeks turn all pink when he smiles at you."

Tam put her hands on Annabel's lap and leaned forward.

"I think you and papa are so in love with each other, you just don't know it."

"I think, you should should go to sleep." Annabel playfully put her hand on Tams face and pushed her back into her pillow. The girl erupted in a fit of giggles that Annabel tried to shush so her other two siblings sharing the room won't wake up.

"Good night mama."

"Good night my darling." Annabel kissed her cheek and got up, turning the lamp off and quietly slipping out of the room.

"So we haven't kissed?" Someone whispered from behind her.

Annabel jumped in surprise and put a hand over her heart.

"You startled me!" She whisper shouted at Richard. "And no, we haven't."

She started to walk towards her room and Richard followed close behind her.

"I think you need me to re-jog your memory." He cheekily grinned at her. She stopped dead in her tracks and glared back at him.

"I'm kidding. Making out doesn't count as kissing." He wiggled his eyebrows and she huffed and turned around, continuing her walk to her room.

"We both agreed that we will forget that ever happened." She said. He fell into step with her and slipped his hand in hers, and when she didn't pull away he intertwined their fingers and grinned.

"Wipe that grin off your face Pelton."

"How can you even tell I'm grinning. The hallway's so dark you can barely see four steps in front of you."

"I just know. Anyways, this is me. Good night." She let go of his hand and opened her door. She stepped in her room and was about to close the door when Richard called out to her. "Yes?"

He leaned down and placed a tender kiss on her lips.

"There, now we can say we kissed."

He narrowly dodged her slipper being flung at him and he ran to his room, a laugh bubbling up from deep within his chest.

With flushed cheeks, Annabel slammed her door shut, but at the last second, closed it gently as to not wake anyone up.

This was the second time they kiss. The first was in the hotel in Switzerland, although that was more making out than a kiss, and the second was just now. They had promised each other that they would forget what happened in Switzerland and continue as if nothing happened at all. It was unprofessional for her to continue being the childrens nanny while they kissed or harboured any feelings for each other. So the second they arrived back home, she's been working on pushing her feelings deep deep down and they were on the verge of resurfacing and overwhelming her. Not just that, but the kids haven't been of any help either. If Maggie hadn't said that blasted comment then Richard wouldn't have kissed her again, she knew it. And what Tam told her moments ago got her mind and heart racing. She didn't know what to make of it. It was absurd of her to think that Richard had any feelings towards her, someone of the lower classes, someone of lower standards. And she knew the first kiss between them was just in the heat of the moment and the second one was just joking around. It must be that. Richard Pelton no way had any feelings for her.

As soon as Richard entered his room, his laughing came to a stop and the smile on his face dropped. He was screwed. He was screwed ten times over and that's all because he fell in love with his own childrens care taker. He wanted nothing more than to hold her and properly kiss her. Not give her a peck on the lips or a rushed kiss. No, he wanted to make her feel loved and cherished.

He paced the length of his room as thought after thought invaded his mind.

He loved Annabel so bad that it now hurt his heart to ever think of a life without her. Except he could do nothing about his love for her. She didn't reciprocate his feelings. She probably hated him now because he stole another kiss from her, without her permission, again. How could she even fall in love with him when he still had a slight limp? When she's a person that deserves someone even better than him? Why would she ever want to settle down with a man that already has a family? He knew she loved the children, but if they do end up getting married, which is highly unlikely, would she still love them as her own children? Would his children accept her as their own mother? They already call her mama, but what if it was official? Would they still? He knew his thinking was getting him nowhere and that he should stop. But thought after thought, self doubt after self doubt swarmed his head and sunk their claws into his brain and no matter how hard he tried, he couldn't shake them out.

He got into bed and settled with the idea of just remaining as respectful as he can towards her and focus on the coming up event instead.

Christmas

"**W**ake uuuuuuuppppp!" Sam screamed at the top of his lungs in the foyer while Tam and Margot banged on everyone's doors.

"It's Chwistmas!" Margot said loudly as she banged on Maggie's door which flung open, revealing a very happy Maggie, who would have normally been very cross with the child for waking her up like that. But it was Christmas.

Christmas was an exception.

"Let's go wake up mama and papa!" Maggie picked up her younger sister and twirled her around as she laughed.

"No need. We're already awake." Annabel said as she and Richard walked down the hallway to them.

"You're still in your sleep wear." Maggie said, a grin stretching far across her face. She kissed both Annabel's and her papas cheeks in greeting and Margot copied her.

"So are you. I believe Christmas is an exception to wearing sleepwear in the morning, don't you think?" Annabel said, taking Margot from Maggie's arms as they all headed down together.

"So you and papa woke up at the same time. Did you also..."

Annabel slapped Maggie upside the head and the girl ran away giggling.

"Good morning sir." Mr.Peltons butler greeted everyone, he was also in his pajamas, and so was every other staff member.

"Should we have breakfast first?" George asked as everyone went into the large living room where they had their Christmas tree set up.

"We do always have breakfast first." Maggie agreed, although she felt a little sad.

Every year they ask their father to have breakfast after opening presents, but he never allowed that.

The children got up from their seats and dejectedly headed to the dinning room.

"Children. We'll have breakfast after opening presents." Annabel said and took a seat on the single couch.

"But papa always says-"

"Well, I don't think he really minds this time. Do you Mr.Pelton?" She asked him and gave him a certain look that said to not even try saying that he minded.

"No, not at all." He said and also made his way over to the couches.

The children looked at each other with excitement and ran back to the couches and sitting under the Christmas tree.

"Me first! Can I go first?" Margot said and they all agreed. Margot still couldn't read properly, but she knew that M was for Margot, so she took all the presents that had an M at the beginning.

"These ones are mine Mar Mar." Maggie laughed and took the ones with her name.

"M for Margot." Margot argued.

"M is also for Maggie." Maggie flicked her nose.

"But M is for Margot! G is for Gigi." Margot's bottom lips trembled and tears pricked her eyes.

"Now now Margot. Look here. This is how you spell Margot and this is how you spell Maggie. We both have an M in our name." Maggie said, trying to calm her down before she started to cry.

"Okay." And then Margot forgot about the confusion and ripped through her presents.

After Margot, no one was patient enough to wait their turn, so they all just opened theirs up.

Annabel sat back and watched everyone open everything with a smile on her face.

"Are you not going to open yours?" Richard asked.

"Mine? I'm not expecting any." She looked at him with slight confusion. He tilted his head towards the kids and when she turned to look, she gasped.

They were standing there, holding out a present for her.

"It's for me? But you guys didn't have to get me anything."

"You gave each of us something, it's only right we give you one. Plus, we all made it." Sam said.

"I hope you like it." Tam said. She took the present out of her siblings hands and placed it on Annabel's lap.

"That's very thoughtful of you. I'm really great full." She held a hand out for them and they each leaned down and she kissed their cheek.

"Open it up!" Maggie excitedly said. They sat down right in front of her, their eyes opened wide with excitement.

"Alright." Annabel laughed and opened up the present.

She smiled warmly at the painting they had created of her favorite meadow.

"We noticed that you really like to sit out in the back meadow where the horses graze. So we painted it for you." Maggie grinned.

"I really love it, thank you from the bottom of my heart." She gave them all a big group hug.

"But look here, Tam messed this horse up." Sam pointed to a deformed horse that wasn't noticeable until pointed out.

"I told you that was Margot, not me!" Tam shoved him away and stuck her tongue out.

"It doesn't matter, I think it makes the painting all better. Tam, apologise to Sam because you pushed him." Annabel said and steadied Sam.

She apologised to him and another present dropped in her lap.

"Imadeyousomethingextra." George said, slightly embarrassed. This was the first time he gifts her anything and he really hopes that she likes it.

"Hey! We said we'd all do the painting. This is cheating!" Maggie glared at her brother but he avoided her gaze and just studied Annabel's reaction as she opened it.

Maggie didn't like that George was winning the race to being Annabels favorite.

"Oh George! It's quite lovely. Did you carve it yourself?" Annabel gushed over it and turned it around in her hands to look at all the sides.

"Yes."

"Thank you. I'm going to keep this forever." She got up from her seat and gave him a proper hug and a kiss on the cheek.

He had carved out a squirrel that looked almost exactly identical to the one she saved half a year ago.

"Papa? Did you get anything for mama?" Tam said and bounded over to her father.

"Now Tam, we don't go around aski-" Annabel began to say because she didn't want Tam to pressure Richard into saying anything since he hadn't gotten her anything.

"I did actually."

"You did?" Annabel turned to look at him with surprise.

"I did." He pulled out a small velvet box from his pocket.

Maggie and George gasped.

"George, is this really happening?" She whispered to her older brother as they stood there in utter shock.

"It's small and I didn't know how to wrap it, so..." He got up and headed towards her. "I hope you like it darling."

He gave her a soft smile and handed her the velvet box. She felt immense relief that this wasn't a proposal like her and the children's crazy minds thought it was.

"Y-you really didn't have to get me any-" she gasped when she saw the inside. "It's wonderful Richard, but I can't take this." She got up and handed it back to him.

"No no, I got it for you. I want you to have it."

They were standing so close to each other but they haven't even noticed.

"But i-it's too expensive. A-are you sure?"

"Do you reckon they're going to kiss?" Maggie whispered to George.

"Should we shove papa from behind to get them to kiss?" He whispered back at her.

"I'm more than sure." Richard picked up the necklace from its place in the velvet box.

"Turn around Anna." He softly said.

She looked up into his eyes and hesitantly turned around, lifting the hair from off her back so the nape of her neck was exposed.

Richard put the necklace gently around her neck and tried to clasp it but was having a hard time. He leaned down so he had a better look at the clasp and when George and Maggie were too busy whispering to each other and the younger kids were preoccupied with their presents, he placed a quick but tender kiss on the back of her neck.

Annabel dropped her hair in surprise and spun around.

"Thank you. It's really beautiful. Also sorry, I didn't mean to hit you with my hair."

"It's alright." His eyes dropped to where the necklace hung from her neck. He picked up the pendant and brushed it with his thumb, looking at Annabel with such care that even Margot understood.

"It's looks good on you." He smiled and then placed it down.

"You have good taste." She countered.

They stared into each other's eyes for a few more seconds that were far longer than necessary before they snapped out of it and each went to their own seats.

Maggie groaned and then went back to opening her presents when nothing too exciting happened.

As the initial excitement of opening presents died down and hunger settled in, they moved along to the dinning room where a large Christmas breakfast awaited them. They had breakfast with all of the staff and the dinning room was a lot more lively than usual.

Everyone just had a great day which got even better when Mr.Wilton and his kids came for a visit during the late afternoon and stayed well into the evening. His wife couldn't make it. Tiffany and George were teased endlessly for being really close to each other and were forced to kiss because they were standing under the mistletoe. And it was clear as day that this wasn't the first time they kissed.

"Have a great night everyone and merry Christmas." Richard said, walking the Wilton's to the door when it was nearly midnight. Annabel has already herded his younger children to bed and Maggie followed soon after. George was just making his way up and after half an hour of just sitting in the calm silence, Richard too made his way to his room.

This was the first Christmas without his late wife that was actually fun. He prayed she was doing well up in heaven and that she was looking down and smiling at how wonderful her children were growing up to be. And he hoped that she was happy for him for moving on and finding someone that made him so incredibly happy and feel young and alive.

Thinking of Annabel always just put a smile on his face. He had secretly wished that she get him something for Christmas, but he wasn't too sad that she hadn't. Why would she?

He reached his door and opened it up, he stepped in but stubbed his toe at something he didn't see was laying on the ground. He peered down and a huge grin adorned his face. It was a present and it had his name on it, it didn't say who it's from, but he's not stupid, he could recognise that handwriting anywhere.

It was from Annabel, he was sure.

He picked up the box and closed the door after him. He sat on his bed and feeling like a little kid, he ripped through the wrapping and tape to see what's inside. He pulled out thermal pants and some sort of cream. A note tumbled out and he read it.

I read somewhere that if you had an injury and it hurts in the cold (like yours does), it's best to keep it warm and comfortable. So I hope the pants and medical cream are of some service. I also hope you like your new fuzzy socks!

He looked into the box and sure enough, there was a pair of funny fuzzy holiday socks that would surly make anyone laugh if they saw it. He smiled at her thoughtfulness and made a mental note to put them on tomorrow to make her happy.

He went to sleep that night feeling the happiest he's ever felt.

Bonus: New Years (short chapter)

✱ Events in this chapter do not actually happen in the main story line.
   This is just a bonus chapter that you can skip if you want and it won't affect anything. Contents in this chapter will not be brought up in the main story line. This chapter is just for reader enjoyment.

"The whoooole day?" Sam asked as he peered up at his father with big eyes.

"Yes, now go get changed or we'll have less time to have fun." Richard ruffled his sons hair.

"Okay!" Sam ran up the stairs and into his and his sisters room to get changed.

"Mama can you help me?" Tam asked as she tried pulling her pants on.

"I think you can do it on your own Tam. You're a big girl now, and you don't need my help in everything." Annabel said as she assisted Margot with her socks.

"But you're helping Margot."

"Well, Margot is only three and still has a really hard time with her socks. Other than that, Margot can almost dress herself perfectly well. And Sam can dress himself too. If you're really stuck, I will help you, but it seems to me that you have everything under-no, you can't put two legs in one leg hole. This leg goes, yes like that. See, you can do it."

"Yeah! I got it!" Tam cheered.

The three children finished getting changed and headed down to the door where everybody was waiting for them.

Today was the last day of the year and Mr.Pelton told his children that they were going to spend the entire day out in the city and then go to watch the fireworks at midnight. He even gave all his staff the day off. Most of them will also be spending their day in the city.

"Why haven't you dressed?" Richard asked Annabel when she had brought the children down. She wasn't wearing weather appropriate clothes for the snow outside.

"Oh, I wasn't planning on coming along." She politely said. She was so apart of their day to day activities and lives that he got used to the idea of her just being there with them, he didn't think that she'd also maybe just relax on the day off and not tag along, which, if he was being true to himself, upset him a little.

"Why's that?" George asked as he laced up his boot.

"We'd like you to come with us." Maggie said.

"That's very kind of you, but I thought of spending New Years here, at home where it's all nice and warm."

Richard didn't know if he was supposed to be happy because she finally called this place home, or urge her to come along.

"Well, it is everybody's day off, so I can't ask you to come along and help with the children, but I can ask you to just come along. It's going to be a lot of fun." Richard said, hoping she does agree. But he also knew how much she hated the cold and how today was supposed to be one of the coldest days this winter.

"I'd love to, but it would be too cold for me. You all go and have fun. And when you come back, you tell me all about the fireworks." She said and walked with them all the way to the car waiting for them. She watched them get in, shivering in the cold, and the second the car started to pull away, she hurried back inside to the warmth of the house.

*

"Are you going to kiss a random lady at midnight or...?" George asked his father. He knew exactly what he was doing.

Richard stayed quit and felt his mood slightly dampen at the thought that Annabel wasn't with them. She had been on his mind all day and even more since it was nearing midnight. Only half an hour left and they were already at the heart of the city where activities were set up for kids and a viewing area was for the fireworks. His younger kids were being accompanied by Maggie in the toys section, so he didn't have to worry about them.

"You can just go back to her." George continued to say.

"I'm not leaving the kids alone." Richard came up with an excuse.

"They'll be with me and Maggie."

"That's still not bei-"

"Father," George began to say.

Richard froze and looked at his son. He only called him father if he was being very serious.

"I don't know why I have to keep telling you to go after the women you love. If you keep denying your feelings for her, she might find someone else. And by the time you act upon your feelings, it would have been too late."

"I don't love her George."

"Sure, and the grass isn't green. You keep telling yourself that, but it is clear to everybody that has ever seen the two of you interact that you two are in love. It's clear as day, you love her, she loves you. There's nearly 20 minutes until midnight, just enough time to get home. You do what you want with that information." George kept himself rooted to the ground and staring forward while he felt his father staring at him for a good half a minute before leaving. The second his father left, his shoulders slumped and he slightly smiled. That was another step forward in to getting the two of them together.

*

Richard rushed home and when he killed the engine of the car, he only had ten seconds before midnight.

He ran into the house, all the lights were turned off, so that must mean she's in her room. He took the stairs two at a time and knocked on her door.

"Annabel?" He called out.

"Richard?" She opened the door, confused. "You're home earlier than I expected. It's not even midn-"

She suddenly realised what he was doing right in front of her room, before midnight, out of breath and no children in sight.

They stared into each other's eyes as the last seconds of the year ticked away to the New Year. Sounds of firework explosions were heard in the distance and they began to close the distance between each other.

Richard held her hips while she put her arms around his neck and they deeply kissed.

"Happy New Years darling." He pulled back and gently whispered.

"Happy New Years." She murmured back and connected their lips again while he began to walk forward into the room.

Midterms and the Letter

As the winter holidays came to an end, most children in the country were getting ready to take their midterm exams, and the Pelton children were no exception.

George was under a lot of stress, seeing that this was his last high school year before going off to university. His midterms were a big deal. Maggie's exams were also stressful since her grades start to truly count now, seeing that she is in year 10 (grade 9). And although the twins did have some sort of tests being handed out to them at their very young age, they still had it a lot easier than their older siblings. And Margot, she just brought paintings home.

Almost like any other household, Mr.Peltons house was nearly dead silent with the children studying in the library, but the tension and stress was loud enough to deafen any person.

In their immense sense of concentration, Annabel and Richard left the children alone most of the time, seeing them only during meal times and during times they were taking a breather to complain about the amount of studying they have to do. Annabel and Richard did occasionally get called in to help with understanding or to test the children on certain subjects, but other than that, the children didn't want anyone with them. It got too stressful like that.

"A letter for you Annabel." Samantha handed Annabel her letter, she was the one that got the mail today.

"Thank you Samantha." She took the letter from the womens hand, and with Margot holding her other hand, they walked into Richards office.

"Aren't you two just a sight for sore eyes." He smiled up at them and leaned back in his chair, putting down the papers he was looking at. His smile only grew when Annabel shot him a look. "Hey Mar." He picked his daughter up on to his lap when she came around his desk to give him the wet stick she found outside.

"It's wonderful, thank you." He kissed the top of her head and opened up one of his drawers to reveal that it was filled with sticks. He added the new one to the ever growing collection and placed Margot down to go play with the few toys he allowed inside his office.

"What do you have there?" He said, getting up from his seat and heading to the couch where Annabel was sitting.

"It's a letter from my mothers neighbor in the flat next door. Why is she..." As Annabel's eyes scanned the contents of the letter, her face turned from its natural, slightly flushed cheeks to a ghostly white and her hands began to slightly tremble.

"What's wrong?" Richard sat down and took the letter from her hands and began reading while she just sat there, clamping her hands together and thinking up the worst possible scenarios.

"W-what do I- I." She began to say once he put the letter down.

"You need to go to her." Richard said and folded the letter back up while studying her face.

"But what about the children? They have exams coming up and they might need me, but my mother, she's really sick and I need to be with her. But if I leave you and the chi-"

"Annabel, it's okay. Just calm down." He took her hands in his and moved closer.

She stopped rambling and felt a small sense of safety and security just from him holding her hands.

"We'll be okay. You don't have to worry about us. I'll help the children if they need anything with their school work. And Sam and Tam are getting more independent, no need to stress over them. You need to go to your mother and focus on her. She needs you right now. Stay with her for as long as you need."

"A-are you sure? Won't the children-"

"They'll understand. And anyways, this time it's an emergency and you are coming back, so it will all be okay."

"Okay, okay. I'll, um, I'll go and pack and then I'll take the train, and, oh, I'll just get going." She hurriedly got up, Richard following her lead and she rushed to the door.

"Oh,umm, Richard?" She stopped from stepping out and looked back at him.

"Yes darling?"

She ran back to him and hugged him tight.

He stood surprised for a second before hugging her back. He did have to lean slightly down, but it was perfect. She was perfect. It felt as if they were molded for each other. He closed his eyes, really feeling the hug before all to soon, she began pulling back.

"Annabel," he called out when she was at the door again. "if you need anything, just give me a call. I'll be there, right beside you."

She could feel his sincerity with every word he said.

"You'll be the first one I reach out to if I need help." She promised him and then hurried to her room.

"Mama! I'd like some help!" George called out to her as she went down the hall to her room. She went to the railing and looked down to where he was standing beside the large library door.

"I'd love to George, but I have a train to catch and not much time."

"A train? What for?"

"Well, you tell me what a train is used for Georgie."

"Alright alright. Where are you headed and for how long?"

"I'm heading back home to my mother. But I'll be back soon."

"Is she alright?"

"There's no need to worry." She smiled at him and went to pack her clothes. She didn't want to worry him while he has exams to study for.

"What's going on with mama?" George said, barging in to his fathers office.

"Whatever do you mean?" Richard asked, he wasn't sure how much Annabel told them. So he didn't want to tell them something she didn't. "Next time, please knock on the door."

"She's going to visit her mother."

"And what's wrong with that?"

"Normally, nothing. But when she was working for Mr.Wilton, he gave her a week break to go visit her. And now winter break is over, so it doesn't make sense why she's leaving now, especially with exams coming up. Why does she have to go see her again?"

"Last I checked, Annabel isn't taking any exams so she doesn't need to worry about them." Richard said, going back to his work so he would come off as uninterested.

"Why'd you let her go?"

"Well, since she's worked for me, I haven't given her anymore than a few days off and that's unfair. And she wants to visit her mother again, so why not?"

George just sighed and left to go study again.

Richard could understand why Annabel didn't tell George the real reason as to why she's leaving, she doesn't want them to worry right before their exams.

He heard the sound of running feet on the second floor and recognized them as Annabel's, although they were heavier this time which meant that she was carrying her suit case. He beckoned Margot over when he reached his office door so they could see her off.

Tam was balling her eyes out by the door. Tears streaked down Sams face. Maggie was holding in her tears and George was nowhere to be found.

"I promise you all, I will be back as soon as I can. Now you must promise me to work extra hard and try your very best in your studies. Don't cause any unnecessary trouble for papa and be sure to eat your entire meals, alright?" She crouched down and wiped Tams tears, pulling her into a tight hug.

"No need to cry Tami. I'll be back. And I'll call as much as I can."

"You promise?"

"Of course." Annabel pulled away and Sam also hugged her. And then she got up and hugged Margot and Maggie. Richard was debating with himself whether he should hug her again or not, and when he noticed that she too was on the verge of tears falling down her face, he pulled her into a hug. He wrapped his arms around her waist tightly and she slightly went up on her toes and put her arms around his neck and her chin on his shoulder.

"Annie...if you need anything, and I mean anything, just call. Even if you just want someone there with you." He whispered to her. Reminding her that he was here for her.

She replied by leaning into him more. She felt completely safe in his arms. Like nothing from the outside world could hurt her if she just stayed where she was, with him. Like anything was possible as long as the two of them were together.

They pulled back and Annabel felt better, a lot more calm after that hug.

"I'll see you all soon." She said one last time before she was out the door.

Maggie was going to say a cheeky comment to her father, but saw the amount of sadness in his eyes that she just let it go.

"You can go now Phil." Annabel said to Phil who was in the drivers seat and who would usually be taking care of the horses, but today he was driving her to the train station because the driver twisted his ankle.

"Hold on." George said from the outside. He reached for the door and got in, joining Annabel in the back seats. "I'm coming with you."

Annabel studied his face for a second before reaching over and taking hold of his hand.

"Alright."

If George was surprised that she agreed so easily, he didn't show it, instead, he held on to her hand tighter, almost seeming like he was too scared to let go.

Annabel could understand what George was going through right now. He's already lost his birth mother, and he was old enough to still have many memories of her when she past away. So he must miss her dearly and her passing must have affected him more than he let on. The first time she's seen him be a huge emotional wreck was when she first left. And now the second time, although he wasn't screaming out and crying like last time, he was trying to calm his self at the thought of having his mother go, all over again. This must be very scary for him and he was probably be very doubtful that she will be coming back.

"I'll be back." She said for reassurance when they were nearly there.

"But what if you don't?"

"Why would I not?"

"I don't know, but what if-"

"What if you stop thinking the worst thing is going to happen? Why don't we take this one step at a time?"

"Is she sick? Your mother I mean."

Annabel sighed and pulled her hand away. She thought that he at least should know the truth.

"Terribly so."

"And there's no one else that can help her?"

"No, my father and brother have already past away and our neighbors are too busy to help out."

"I'm sorry for your loss."

"It's alright, it wasn't your fault now was it?" She grinned at him although she was hurting on the inside.

"May I ask how they past away?"

She softly smiled at his curiosity and looked out the window.

"Blasted Germans did it. My father got chemical gassed, more than half of his squad or whatever you call it, couldn't make it. And my brother, Adam, he got shot."

"They're war hero's."

"They sure are. So that's why I have to go back to my mother. I need to help take care of her until she's better."

"And what if..."

"Let's hope not."

Taking Care of Mum

Annabel was the first off the train when it came to a stop. She saw a few familiar faces in the little city they lived in but she couldn't stay and chit chat, just a quick hello and how have you been's sufficed.

Outside of her mothers apartment door, she took a few deep breaths to calm herself and so she wouldn't startle her mother if she busted in like a maniac.

The door opened and their neighbours was standing there.

"Gosh you startled me! I didn't think you'd come this quick." Mrs.Smith quickly glanced behind her and shut the door so she could talk to Annabel without her mother listening in.

"I-is she okay? How bad?"

"I got the doctor to come out and take a look at her. He doesn't know what's wrong, just that she's very very sick. She's sleeping now in her bed, but she's a cheeky little one and I believe she's faking it just so I could leave and so she could get up."

"Did he say anything about her getting any better?"

"He doesn't know, because he's never seen this illness before."

"Well surly someone has. I'll call all the doctors in this city. Someone must know."

"Dear, even if they did...she, she doesn't have that long."

"W-what?" Annabel's head spun and she held on to Mrs.Smiths shoulder to steady herself.

"I'm sorry. If she continues like this, the high fever will start shutting down her own organs and...well, it's better if you see for yourself. Oh, do you have a cloth? It's best to tie it around your nose and mouth. We don't know if what she has is contagious or not." Mrs.Smith tugged on the cloth around her neck that she had pulled down when she stepped out of the apartment.

"I do, thank you for looking after her until I got her."

"Of course. She's my dear friend." And with that, Mrs.Smith went to her apartment next door and Annabel walked into her mothers.

She put her stuff in her room and took a cloth, tying it around her face to cover her nose and mouth. She took another deep breath and walked into her mothers room, taking a seat on the chair by her bed. She studied her mothers pained face, how red it was, sweat dribbling down her forehead. She didn't have a blanket covering her because of how bad she was burning up. Her skin was blotched in tones of yellow and a deep ugly purple. Her hair was sticking to her head and her clothes to her body. Annabel brought a large bowl of cold water, filled with ice cubes and dipped a cloth in it before placing it on her mothers forehead.

"I'll take care of you now, you just rest and focus on getting better."

She took a few more towels and placed them along her mothers arms to help in cooling her down.

Her mother didn't wake up until a few hours later when the sun was beginning to set.

"Annabel?"

"Mother," Annabel said, feeling very glad that she had finally woken up, she was getting worried that she was sleeping for too long. "How are you feeling?"

"What are you doing here?"

"Are you not happy to see me?" She asked playfully.

"It's just, I saw you a few weeks ago."

"I can really feel the love mother." She rolled her eyes but was smiling, happy that her mother feels good enough to be sarcastic.

"How do I look?" Her mother asked, she couldn't really lift herself up to see her discolored body.

"Like the lates fashion trend." Annabel said, picking up the towel off her head and putting it back in the bowl, ringing it, and putting it back.

"That bad, huh?"

"You're going to be okay." She swallowed the lump in her throat, scared that her words might not be true at all.

"What have I always taught you?"

"To never make promises you're not sure you can keep."

"Yes, exactly." Her mother took hold of her hand and patted it. "I know you want me to be okay, but..."

"I made some soup, I'll go get you some. You must be hungry." Annabel quickly said and got up. She didn't like where her mothers sentence was going and decided to change the topic. She hurriedly left the room to get a bowl of soup ready for her mother, and after collecting herself and taking a few deep breaths she went back in.

"You know we're going to have to talk about it." Her mother said immediately.

"I don't want to."

"The doctors don't even know what's wrong with me. I'm sleeping more and more, we both know it's coming."

"I refuse to believe it."

"How are the children?" Her mother changed the subject once she realized she really won't be able to get her to talk about it.

"They're okay. George and Mr. Pelton share their regards with you and wish you a smooth and speedy recovery." Annabel propped her mother up and supported her by placing pillows behind her.

"Ah yes, Richard. How is he? Have you two started planning your weeding yet?"

Annabel sighed and started feeding her some of the soup.

"You really need to stop saying that and getting your hopes up. Mr.Pelton and I are never going to work out."

"And why's that?"

"Look at me mother. And look at him. We're both from two completely different worlds. He needs a strong women by his side, someone that he and his children will love and someone that will get accepted by the society they are in. Not a nanny."

"Last time I checked, all humans came from earth. Unless he's from Mars or something, then I still think you stand a chance. And since when did you look down on the job you loved so much?"

"You know what I mean when I say two different worlds. And I do love my job. It's just...why would he want someone like me to be by his side?"

"Why would he not? You're an amazing women Annabel, and you deserve to be with the man you love. Forget about what other people think, we don't do what we do to please them. Unless you're an actor or singer, which you're not. Follow your heart...and your nose, follow your nose too. It usually leads to food."

The to women stared at each other before bursting out in laughter.

"But you do love him, don't you?" Her mother asked when they were just calming down.

Annabel sat quietly for a moment. She's always been attracted to Richard Pelton. His built physique, his kind eyes and warm smile. She loved the way he cared and worried for her. She loved that he loved his children and wanted the best for them, and how he always tried his best to make time for them. She loved the way her hand felt in his, how his lips felt on hers, and even the way he would secretly glance at her, thinking she wouldn't notice. There were many many things that made her love him and those were only a few she could immediately think of.

"I-I...do love him." She said and looked down at her hands holding the nearly finished bowl of soup. This was the first time she's ever admitted to loving him, and out loud.

"Good to know I have five grand children before I die." Her mother happily said.

"Mother! This is not something to joke about!" Annabel huffed and stuffed more soup into her mothers mouth.

The Funeral

Annabel's mother didn't last more than five days before she past away and joined her husband and son in heaven. And even though Annabel knew this was going to happen, she wasn't ready, how could she ever be?

"M-mother?" Annabel said, traces of fear lingering in her voice. Her mother was just as she left her moments ago. Sitting up, trying to read the newspaper, with a smile on her face. Except her skin looked ghostly and grey, her eyes were closed, and her fingers weren't holding onto the newspaper anymore, but she was still smiling.

"I know you've been joking about it, but this is taking it too far." Annabel said as tears began welling in her eyes. "Mother?"

She walked forward, bowl of water in her hands as the tears trickled down her face.

"M-maybe you're just sleeping, right?" But she knew her mother was gone when she placed the bowl down on the bed side table and took hold of her ice cold hands to feel for her heart beat.

Annabel collapsed on her mothers lap and cried in pain at losing her mother, her last blood relative. She cried at the pain of losing both her parents and brother, at the pain of never being able to see them again. At never spending time with each other again and making unrealistic plans for their future. At annoying each other. At saying their I love you's. She cried because non of them got a chance to really live their lives to the fullest and were just taken away from the world, from her. And she cried because she didn't have a mother anymore.

Mrs. Smith heard the crying from next door and her heart pained her for the poor girl. She got up and out of her apartment and went over to Annabel who was crying her heart out, clutching at the blanket on top of her mothers lap.

She placed a comforting hand on the young womens shoulder as she too began to softly cry for her lost friend.

*

The funeral was a few days later and opposite of everyone's sad and mourning mood, the sky was as bright and sunny as could be, with only a few white fluffy clouds offering some shade.

Annabel was barely able to get through saying what she had to say with a never ending stream of tears rolling down her face. And although she was sad and heartbroken, she really felt the love of everyone that had come for her mother. They all were close to her mother and loved her just as much as she did.

As they lowered her mother deep into the earth, a sinking, suffocating feeling grew inside of her and she wasn't sure if she will ever be able to get out of it. There was a constant lump in her throat that made it so it was more difficult to breath and talk and it didn't show any signs of going away.

She stood next to the grave for a long time after, her mind was just blank, but the lump and suffocation was still there.

Annabel eventually made it back to the apartment and she immediately began packing her mothers things. Anything that she wore during the time she was sick had to be burned as to not spread whatever she had, that included her comforter, sheets and blanket. Then she got to packing the things for charity, which was nearly everything. The only thing that Annabel kept was their few family pictures that they had of all of them together, her mothers jewelry and her scarf that she loved very much. She also kept the few things they had of her brothers and fathers belongings, which included their dog tags and a few items that were of value to them.

A knock on the door pulled her out of her cleaning trance and she dragged herself to the door.

"Need any help?" Mrs. Smith said, offering a kind, yet sad smile. Mrs.Smith sat in the front with Annabel during the funeral, holding her hand the entire time.

"I'm nearly finished." Annabel said in a very quiet voice. She stepped aside and let the older women in. All she had to do was scrub the apartment clean and give the keys back to the landlord.

Mrs.Smith quietly began helping with scrubbing the house down and taking all the boxes out, her husband, Mr.Smith, came in later and offered to take the burnables to the dumpster, which Annabel was glad for. Even though she knew she had to burn them, she didn't have the heart to do it herself.

The next day she and Mrs.Smith were able to give the charity boxes to homeless shelters which made Annabel feel a little better, because she knew that's what her mother would have wanted. Her mother was a kind soul that loved helping everyone. Lots of people at the funeral had talked about her endless kindness.

"How long are you staying for?" Mrs. Smirh asked once they reached the apartment.

"I'm leaving this evening."

"Oh, so soon?"

"I can't stay here anymore."

"I understand."

"Mrs.Smith..." Annabel called out when the older women was making her way to the door. She stopped and looked back. "Thank you, for everything. And for being her good friend and keeping her company when I couldn't. I know this must be hard for you too."

"This is life. People come and go. Your mother told me about Richard. I don't know when I'll be seeing you again, so, if he really makes you happy and he's it for you, don't let him go Annie." Mrs.Smith gave her a warm smile and headed out the door.

Annabel sighed and slumped into a kitchen chair, she has to call Richard and tell him that's she's coming back home. She hasn't called since her mother passed.

"Oh, one more thing dear," Mrs.Smith popped her head back in the door way, "don't forget to invite us to the wedding."

"O-okay." Annabel didn't have enough energy to tell her that Mr.Pelton probably didn't want to marry her, or be in a relationship with her.

When Mrs.Smith left again, Annabel went over to the phone and reached for it with slightly trembling hands. She dialed the Peltons number and waited for someone to pick up.

"Ummm hi. I'm Margot."

For some reason, hearing Margot's voice made Annabel want to break down into tears all over again.

"H-hey Mar Mar." She said trying to hold onto a sob. "Can you get papa for me?"

"Ah! Mama! You didn't call for a week."

"I'm sorry. I'm really sorry." Tears ran down her face and she was stuttering in her breathing. "P-please get papa."

She pulled the phone away and calmed herself down by taking very deep breathes and putting a hand over her heart to put pressure and ease the sudden waves of pain.

"Annabel, darling. How's your mother doing?" She heard Richards voice and tried to keep her bottom lips from trembling.

"Richard..."

Just in the way she said his name, he knew. His heart broke for her and he wanted nothing more than to be with her and wrap her up in his arms.

"Sh-she's-"

"Would you like me to come over?"

She wanted to say yes, but what's the point if she's coming back this evening?

"No, it's alright. I'm coming back this evening. Just thought I'd let you know."

"I'll be waiting at the station then."

"You don't have to." He didn't have to, but she wanted him to.

"I want to."

Annabel sunk down on the floor and pressed her back onto the wall, brining her knees up and resting her head on them as her body shook with silent sobs.

Richard sat on the ground and leaned against the wall. He didn't like her being sad and heart broken. Not at all. He didn't like that he couldn't do anything to make her feel better. He leaned his head back, still holding up the phone and sighed.

"I wish I were there with you." He whispered so quietly he was sure the phone didn't pick it up.

"Me too."

Broken But Back Home

Annabel sat quietly on the entire train back home. She didn't utter a single word, not to the man collecting the tickets, and not to the couple sitting in front of her asking if she was okay. She was oblivious to the world around her and she longed to be in Richards safe and secure arms; fully knowing that she didn't have the right, as his employee, to want to be in them, but she did. She just wanted to be wrapped up in a big warm hug and never be let go of.

Hours later, and after many stops and switching to other trains, it was finally time for Annabel to get off. The couple that were sitting in front of her and shared all the destinations with her shared worried glances at the state she was in. They really hoped she would be okay. The man got up and helped in bringing her bags down from the over head compartment and after a very very quiet thank you, she grabbed her stuff and left.

Richard sat waiting at the train station hours before it was supposed to arrive. Maybe she had gotten the time wrong? But he knew that deep down he thought if he came early, then maybe she would also magically come back early. He anxiously watched his wrist watch's big hand tick away in anticipation, and just as it ticked to the time the train was supposed to arrive, a train whistle had him up and out of his seat.

He watched as people piled out of the train, looking for his person. His person that really needed him right now. And just like he was somehow drawn to her, he turned around from where he was searching, in the other direction, and his eyes immediately found her, and although she looked tired and worn out, he still found her to be the most beautiful thing he's ever seen.

"Annabel..."

He weaved through the ever growing crowd on the platform to make his way to her and just like how randomly his head snapped in her direction, hers did too. She was looking down when she suddenly looked up and locked eyes on him amidst the evening crowd.

"Richard..."

She left her bags on the ground and took the last few steps to meet him before crumbling in his arms. He protectively wrapped his arms around her somewhat smaller body, both of them nestling their noses in the others neck.

"I'm here." He mumbled when he felt the tears wetting his neck and shirt. "I'm here for you."

She just nodded and they stayed embracing for a while longer, not caring about the world moving around them.

"Let's go home darling."

"Okay." Her quiet broken voice pulled at his heart strings and he so badly wanted to take her pain away, but he didn't know how to, other than just being there for her and lending an ear if she needed someone to talk to.

He picked up her bags, noticing that she came back with an extra one and they headed to the car parked outside.

The ride back to the house was filled with heavy silence. The type of silence that if you tried to break it, things would just get worse, so they just suffocated quietly.

"I'll bring the bags up to your room, don't bother." He told her once they arrived and all he got was a silent nod.

The children were anxiously waiting for Annabel to come back home. Sam and Tam could understand that she might be really sad once she's back and might not want to talk, but Margot, Margot didn't and she was running around in excitement, which was getting on both George and Maggie's nerves.

"Margot! Will you calm down just a little bit?" George groaned.

"You're all sad. Why?" She asked and stopped her running around to observe her siblings.

"Because Mama is sad." Maggie said.

"How do you know she's sad? Did you see her?" Margot tilted her head to the side. George didn't get a chance to reply because the front door opened and in stepped their mother who they haven't seen for nearly two weeks.

"I'm home." She said quietly and looked at all of them with a soft gaze, but there was no hiding the pain and sadness in her eyes and posture. Margot launched herself at Annabel, and instead of usually catching her and spinning her around in happiness, Annabel just let Margot hang on to her torso, before slipping down her legs and falling on the ground.

"Sorry Mar, I don't feel very good right now." She sadly said, but did affectionatly pat the girls head.

"Are you sick?" Margot asked.

"My heart is, but it will feel better after a few days, I'm sure."

"Mama, come down." Margot mentioned for her mother to crouch down and Annabel couldn't deny the innocent girls request. Once she crouched down, Margot leaned on her knees and placed her ear over Annabel's heart. "I'm a doctor, I will tell you if your heart is sick, oh, it's beating very very fast."

"Yes, it does that sometimes." Annabel got up and faced the rest of the children who had sad expressions on their faces. "And why are you all sad? Did you get in trouble with papa?"

They shook their head no.

"Are you okay mama?" Maggie asked, coming forward.

"I will be."

"Does it hurt your heart?" Sam and Tam asked as they too came up to her and put their arms around her and Maggie.

"It does."

"We'll be here for you." George said, joining in on the group hug.

"Thank you, but I think I'd like to stay alone, just for a little while."

"How long?" Margot asked.

"How long are you willing to give me?" Annabel asked back.

"As long as you need." Richard said from behind, he came up to her and placed a loving kiss on top of her head.

"Thank you every body."

Helping Mama

And just like she said, Annabel has stayed in her room and has not stepped a foot outside. She spends most of her days trying to sleep and trying to sort through her emotions, or, more often than not, from the field outside she could be seen sitting at the window seat and gazing out in to the open with a sort of lost expression on her face.

"It's been five days. Five days!" Sam whailed, "That's it, I'm going in."

"Good luck trying, George and I already did." Maggie dejectedly said. Her and George tried to get Annabel out of the room, but were never successful. It was very hard for all of them to know that their mama was so close yet still out of reach, it was driving them insane.

Sam grabbed Tam by one hand, Margot by the other and marched with them out of the play room and to Annabel's room a few doors over.

"Ready, on the count of three." Sam told his sisters, they both nodded and when he counted down from three, they all screamed at the top of their lungs.

Richard, startled, dropped his pen and ran up the stairs to where his children's screams were. He was just in time to see them walk into Annabels room with big smiles on their faces.

"How are they allowed inside?" He grumbled to himself and went up to the door, only to hear the lock. He groaned and went back downstairs. She didn't even let him in, why did they get to go in? Was screaming the secret password?

"Why did you scream?" Annabel asked and went back to her previous window seat.

"How else would you let us in?" Sam asked and they walked up to her, but it was very very clear that she wasn't doing very well.

Her skin was pale and there was bags under her eyes, and since she's only eaten two meals throughout the entire five days of staying in her room, she was starting to loose weight.

"Mama you're tired?" Margot asked and tried to climb up on Annabel's lap, but Annabel wasn't paying attention to her, she was looking at a butterfly out the door.

"Hmm, isn't it too early for butterflies?" She mumbled and placed a finger on the window, and the butterfly landed on the other side. It lifted one of its legs, placed it on the spot Annabel's finger was on for a few moments, and then took off again.

"Don't climb up Mar. Mama is tired." Tam said and dragged Margot off, only then did Annabel remember that they were in her room.

"You didn't need to scream to get my attention. You could have just asked." She got up and herded them to the door. "Thank you for checking in, don't worry, I will get better." She kissed each of their heads and gently pushed them out the door and locked it behind them.

"We need a plan." Sam said, barging into George's room with his two sisters. Maggie was also there.

"Oh, did you not get in?" She teased.

"We did." Tam said, "but we need to help mama."

"You can't help someone if they aren't willing to accept it." George said from his spot on his desk. He was hunched over a piece of paper.

"What are you doing?" Margot asked.

"Nothing that concerns you."

"So you got in?" Maggie asked, she got up from her laying down position on George's bed.

"Yes, but Mama looks really tired. She has dark circles under her eyes." Sam pulled his cheeks down. "And she looks really white."

"Pale?" George corrected.

"Yes pale." Sam nodded, "and she's skinnier because she doesn't eat."

"I wish I were skinnier." Maggie huffed at her body.

"No Gigi! You look pretty!" Margot gave her older sister two slightly chubby thumbs up.

"Okay, so what's your plan?" George asked and finally turned around, he hid whatever he was working on in his pocket.

"We have to make her happy again!" Tam clapped excitedly. "Mama doesn't eat anything the cooks and Samantha make, so, Maggie, do you want to make cookies with me for mama? Maybe she'll eat it if it's from us?"

"Sure." Maggie got up and held Tams outstretched hand.

"Then Sam and I will make her lunch today." George said and Sam nodded.

"What about me?" Margot said.

"Your job is to keep mama hydrated. She doesn't drink enough water and that's not good." Maggie said.

"Okay! I get mama water." She ran out the room in determination, down the stairs, tripping down the last few, but got up and continued her running to the kitchen.

"Quickly quickly!" She said and it got the maids attention really fast.

"What is it?" Samantha worriedly asked. They thoughts something was horribly wrong.

"I need water."

They all sighed in relief and then one of them gave her a glass of water.

"Okay bye!" She ran out the kitchen, the water spilling left and right and by the time she reached Annabel's room, only a quarter of the water was left.

"Mama! Open the door please!" She shouted and knocked with her little fist.

Annabel slowly opened the door and looked down at the girl who was proudly holding up a glass of quarter filled water.

"Who's this for?"

"You!"

"Oh, thank you." Annabel took the glass out of her hand, and not wanting to upset the girl, drank it all in front of her. She didn't realize how thirsty she was until she drank that small amount. Even though she didn't want to at first.

"Good?" Margot asked

"Good." Annabel replied.

"More?" Margot asked.

"More." Annabel said.

"Okay bye!" Margot took the glass and ran back downstairs. Nearly slipping on the water all over the floor.

Her four older siblings were watching from George's doorway down the hall.

"Okay, good. She'll take what we give her." George said, and when Annabel shut the door again, they all rushed down the stairs to do their tasks.

Annabel wasn't sure what exactly was up with the children. They'd come in pairs and offer her different types of food that they had made themselves, and not wanting to turn them down and make them upset, she always ate it all. It made her happy to see that her actions made them happy. And when she realized what they were doing, she couldn't be more greatful to have them with her. They didn't push her to come out anymore and kept things at her own pace. If she was full, then they would immediately stop, and they always made the food themselves, without any help. She knew because more than half the time it tasted horrible. But she ate it any way. A few days of this and she noticed that she wasn't pale anymore and she looked healthy again and she felt immensely better. She didn't sit sulking throughout the entire day anymore, she looked forward to the children knocking on the door to give her something they cooked or a present they made. She really loved the drawing George made. She even got out of her room to play with the children in their playroom which was an improvement. Her only problem now was sleeping. She couldn't sleep properly no matter how hard she tried. She'd always end up tossing and turning trying to get her dead mother out of her head. Tried getting the thought of never having her again out of her head. She really just wanted to accept it and live on, she didn't want to be stuck in one spot forever.

"We've decided to have lunch with you today." Maggie said when Annabel opened the door when she knocked.

All the children walked into the room with their plates of food and made a large circle on the ground, inviting Annabel with them. She sat down between Margot and George, who handed her her plate.

"And papa? He knows you're not going to be eating with him?" She asked once they started eating and conversing like a semi normal family would.

"It doesn't matter." Maggie said through a mouthful of food.

"So that's where you were." Richard said from the doorway, he had his plate of food in his hands. "I was so confused when you all got up and left without telling me where. Mind if I join you?"

Although he was talking to his children, he never let his gaze wonder from Annabel, this was the first time he sees her in nearly two weeks. He walked in when she nodded and took a seat in front of her, between the twins, not able to take his eyes off of her. It felt like he was in an extremely hot desert with no water for many moons, and he's finally spotted a replenishing oasis. It felt good to see her again.

He wanted to ask her how she's been, but he didn't want to break the cheerful mood everyone was in and instead, enjoyed seeing his children laugh and her genuinely smiling.

*

After spending time with the children in the kitchen and playroom, Annabel called it a day in the early evening.

Even the staff members were happier to see Annabel out and about, baking cookies and blowing flour at the kids.

She got ready for bed and dressed in her pajama. When she sat on the bed, back pressed against the headboard, she put a pillow between her chest and knees when she pulled them up, and held on to her arms under her bent up knees. She shoved her face into the pillow and a flood of tears rolled down her cheeks.

She had an amazing day, one filled with laughter and love, yet she still couldn't peacefully fall asleep. She couldn't help but think of how pathetic she was being. How pathetic and pitiful she must look to the children and Richard. If only she could get it together and move on. But how could she? How does someone move on? Does moving on mean forgetting? Annabel didn't want to forget. Her mother meant the world to her, even more so when both her father and older brother passed away in World War Two. She wanted to move on but not forget. And didn't know how to because memories of the two of them kept suffocating her from trying to do anything else. They shoved to the front of her mind, fighting for her attention, taking up more space than what was welcome and overstaying their visit. She just couldn't get her mind to rest.

Richard went to Annabel's room when he was done helping the younger kids go to sleep. Although she seemed fine today, he was still worried about her.

"Annabel?" He softly whispered when he gently knocked on the door, he didn't want to wake the kids up.

She didn't reply, but her light was still turned on, so she was awake.

"May I come in my darling?"

He still got no reply which got him to worry even more.

"I'm coming in, alright?"

He tried the door handle and to his relief, it wasn't locked. He stepped in and felt his heart drop at seeing Annabel looking so sad sitting on her bed. She peeked up from over her knees and he saw her tear stained cheeks, and red eyes.

"W-why are you here?" She asked, feeling very embarrassed that he's seeing her cry, again.

"I came to check on you." He said walking closer to her bed.

"Well, I'm doing fine. Can you leave now? I don't want you to see me crying, looking all pathetic." She said the last part with her face back into the pillow, hugging herself tighter.

"I don't think you look pathetic. Crying doesn't make anyone pathetic. It makes us human, don't you think?" He sat down on her bed, close to her.

"Please Richard. I don't want you to see me like this." She mumbled and turned her body away from him.

"Alright." And he got up to leave.

Annabel felt bad for pushing him away when all he wanted to do was help. She wanted to call him back, but bit her tongue. Why would she do that if she just told him to go away?

Suddenly, the lights got turned off and she looked up into the darkness.

"Is this better?" He asked and made his way back to the bed.

More tears flowed down her face at Richards thoughtfulness.

"I don't think you look pathetic," he reached for her hand, "or pitiful." he traced random lines and circles on her palm.

"I don't think you look ugly or horrendous when you're crying." he moved closer to her, "you always look beautiful to me and you always will." he leaned forward and placed a kiss on her head.

"It's hard to lose a loved one, I understand, but please don't forget that I am here for you, always." He reached forward and pulled her in for a hug, wrapping his arms around her balled up body while putting the pillow she was hugging to the side. "Even if you just need me to hold you, or if you just need me to listen. I'll be there."

Annabel looked up at the silhouette of his face that was already looking down at her. She didn't know that it was possible, but she just fell in love even more.

"Thank you." Her voice was quiet but she really meant it.

Richard brought a hand up and brushed the tears away.

"Any time."

He couldn't help it, he leaned down and pressed his lips against hers and kissed her.

Annabel slightly gasped in shock but kissed him back, bringing her hands up and around his neck. Richard gently laid her down on the bed and climbed on top of her, propping his elbow up so he didn't crush her with his weight.

When they both broke the kiss for air, Richard took his shirt and pants off.

"I'm not-"

"I know." He said and laid down beside her, pulling her in close to his body. "I was getting uncomfortable wearing my day clothes for so long."

"Oh, I see."

Her cheeks were burning up at being pressed to his bear chest, but it was comfortable and warm and sturdy.

"Annabel..." he pulled her closer and she snuggled up to his chest, feeling very sleepy.

"Hmm?"

"I really- do you- what I'm saying- ugh, never mind."

"What is it?"

He didn't know if he should tell her and if this was the right time or not seeing the current circumstances. She might see it as him trying to take advantage of her weak mental state or as him confessing as pity to her.

"It's nothing. You should probably get some rest."

"You too."

"Alright."

After a while of silence Annabel spoke up.

"Richard..."

"Hmm?"

"You know, you've kissed me three times now, and I haven't even kissed you once."

"You kissed ba-"

She tilted her head up and kissed him, before quickly pulling away and blushing.

"Woah." He whispered and snuggled into her more. He really wanted to tell her how much he loved her, but he was too scared to.

To say that this was the best night the two of them had was an understatement.

To Charity!

- -

After apologizing to the children for taking so long to get herself together and come out of her room, life went back to normal for the Pelton's. They were all finished with their exams and a new school semester had started.

Richard would more often than not, go into Annabel's room at night so they could sleep together. On the days that he didn't, it was very hard to fall asleep. The two of them would also steal a few kisses from each other throughout the day.

"There are so many boxes being brought in, what did you ord..." Annabel's voice trailed off when she walked into Richards big office only to find Rebeca Von Eckerman sitting in one of the two seats opposite of Richards desk.

"Oh, it's seems like I'm interrupting something." She said and began to walk out.

"Annabel! Wait!" Richard got up from his chair and hurried to her.

"Yes?" She said, still holding the door open. Richard stepped outside and motioned for her to close the door so Rebeca didn't hear what he had to say.

"It's not what you think." He immediately said. She tilted her head in confusion.

"And what is it do you think I'm thinking?"

"Well, you must think that-"

"Richard," she placed a hand on his chest that effectively got him to stop talking and smiled, "why would I think that there's something going on between the two of you if you're both respectfully sitting across from each other, just discussing things? And now I'm pretty sure those are her boxes, right? So she's probably here to return whatever you got her. Really, you had to jump to that conclusion right away, didn't you?" She grinned at his shocked expression.

"Now, go back in there and finish whatever it is you need to finish." She straightened out his collar and patted his chest.

Richard grinned down at her and couldn't help but excitedly peck her lips.

She trusted him. She didn't think the worst of him. She had faith in him. He thinks he fell in love all over again. She was so perfect. He didn't deserve her.

He walked back into the office, his face glowing with happiness.

"All's good?" Rebeca asked hopefully. She didn't want Annabel to get the wrong idea. Yes, she didn't like Annabel when she was with Richard, because she was jealous of her. But now, she wasn't with Richard, so it didn't matter. Her and Richard didn't work out, she hopes that the two of them could.

"Couldn't be better. Now, what were you saying?"

*

"You wouldn't believe who came to the house today." Annabel said as she and Tiffany walked down the street together.

"Tell me." Tiffany excitedly said.

"Rebeca Von Eckerman."

"No!" Tiffany gasped and stopped dead in her tracks.

"Yes." Annabel said and laughed at her friends facial expression.

"What did she want?" They resumed their walking.

"Oh, she was just returning what ever Richard got her when they were together. Imagine my surprise when I saw her though."

"Did you freak out?"

"No, why would I?"

"If I was dating a guy, and I found him with his previous ex, I think I'd get furious."

"Well, Richard and I aren't dating, are we? And it also depends on the situation. There was no need for me to get mad at her."

"Oh, Richard and I aren't dating! But we kiss and sleep together, not that way, and hold hands and just sit and talk about everything and nothing for hours!" Tiffany said in high pitched voice, mocking Annabel.

"Oh shut it Tiffany."

"Honestly, you two need to grow a pair. No one does that if they aren't dating! Just confess already. You both know that none of you would even do these stuff if at least you didn't like each other! I can't believe I'm giving relationship advice to someone who should already be married." She mumbled the last part and Annabel slapped her upside the head.

"You're one to talk. What's the deal with you and George? Have you gotten to making babies yet?" Annabel cheekily smiled and Tiffany gasped really loudly.

"Annabel! How could you just say that!? No! We haven't!"

"You'll get to, really soon." Annabel sung and Tiffany shoved her away.

"I can't believe I'm friends with you." She groaned.

"But here we are." Annabel grinned.

"You know, I don't think I've ever seen you in pants and a sweater before." Tiffany said after a while of them just roaming about.

"You did. At the ski mountain."

"That doesn't count."

"Well, for your information, I do wear stuff other than dresses. Summer is for dresses, winter is for sweaters and pants and spring is for t-shits, tank tops and shorts."

"Only you would assign each season what cloths to wear." Tiffany shook her head back and forth.

"It's very efficient, that way, it's a lot easier to plan what I'm going to wear and to clean my closet out and put in the new seasons clothes."

"We're talking like old ladies. Who even talks about seasonal clothes?"

"Me, now, let's go in there. I need to get some stuff."

"Arts and crafts store?"

"Yes, for the kids."

"Old lady." Tiffany grumbled but went in with her nonetheless.

*

The same time the kids came back from school, Annabel came back from her outing.

"Papa!" Sam said excitedly at seeing their father waiting for them, but Richard didn't greet his children like he always did, instead, he beelined to Annabel who wasn't paying attention to him and talking with Maggie instead.

"Where have you been!?" He grabbed her by the shoulders and looked at her face to see if there were any injuries. Then he scanned her body and turned her around to see if she was hurt anywhere.

"What do you mean? I just headed out."

"But you didn't tell me, and I was so worried when I couldn't find you." The panic in his voice was very evident.

"Didn't Samantha tell you? I asked her to tell you so you wouldn't get worried bec-"

"SMANTHA!" Richard hollered.

"I FORGOT!" She hollered back from the kitchen.

"See, all good. I didn't want to bother you while you were speaking with Rebeca."

George and Maggie gasped.

"Rebeca!?" He asked.

"What was she doing her?" Maggie said.

"It doesn't matter, are you hurt?" Richard asked Annabel, turning her around again and again.

"You've already checked, I'm perfectly fine. I went out with Tiffany to get-"

"Tiffany?" George asked.

"Yes Tiffany, anyways-"

"Wait, why do you care if she headed out with Tiffany?" Richard asked George.

"Because she's his girlfriend, like I was saying, we-"

"Girlfriend!?" Richard shouted and glared at his son.

"Yes, now would you let me-"

"Geooorge." He crossed his arms and starred his son down.

"Would you let me finish talking!" Annabel shouted and everyone immediately froze. She's never shouted before. "Thank you, now, where was I?"

"You were out with Tiffany, George's girlfriend, because..." Maggie helped her out.

"Ah yes, because I wanted to get some arts and crafts supplies for the kids. So there you have it. Rebeca was here, George has a girlfriend and that's amazing, so you will not be hounding him about it later, and I got art supplies without getting hurt. Feeling better? Alright, now let's go eat lunch."

The shock of Annabel shouting hadn't worn off yet, so they all obediently went into the dinning room to have their lunch without uttering a single word.

*

"So what are all the boxes?" Sam asked with a mouthful of food.

"Don't talk with your mouth full of food." Maggie scolded him.

"Stuff Rebeca is returning." Richard said.

"What stuff." Tam asked.

"Clothes, bags, jewelry and stuff." He said, sounding very board.

"What are you going to do with it?" George spoke up.

"Return it to the stores."

"Some stuff won't get accepted back." Maggie pointed out.

"Then I don't know."

"How about charity?" Annabel suggested.

"Good idea." Richard said.

"Can I give some of my toys to charity?" Tam asked.

"Of course you can." Annabel smiled at her.

"I don't want to give my stuff away." Sam pouted.

"That's alright. When you give stuff to charity, it's best that it comes from the heart. So you don't have to." Annabel told him.

After they were finished with their lunch, the children hurried up to their rooms to pick what they wanted to give to charity. George was willing to part with some of his hand carved toys and Maggie wanted to donate her many many hair clips, bows, and elastics, while the twins chose some toys, Sam changed his mind and decided to donate, and Margot picked out some of her drawings. Annabel also took some of Margot's, and Sam's clothes that were too small to wear any more.

"Are you going to take some of my clothes?" Tam asked.

"No, Margot will grow into them."

"And how about Maggie?"

"No, you will grow into them."

"And George?"

"Sam will grow into those."

"And yours?"

"Maggie wanted to pick some of them out for herself."

"And papa?"

"That's up to him. Now, no more questions. Did you put everything in a box?"

"Yes."

"Well done. Can you take it downstairs or do you need help?"

"I can do it!"

"Good for you Tam." Annabel smiled at her and finished taping up the box she had.

They loaded the boot of an entire car and still had to put a few boxes in the back seats with the kids.

"I called up a few stores, they don't mind taking the things back. So we'll go to those first." Richard said as they pulled out of the driveway and headed into town.

They were able to return all the jewelry and most of the bags. Only the dresses that weren't tailor fit for Rebeca were accepted back, which was only three.

The charity organizations were more than happy to have a lot of boxes with elegant dresses handed to them.

"Why were they so happy when we gave them all that stuff?" Sam asked.

"Because it's a very nice thing to receive kindness and help, Sam. Don't you get all glad and happy when someone helps you with your homework or helps clean up the mess of toys you made?"

"Well yes."

"It's the same thing. Doesn't it also make you happy to help others?" She smiled down at him and they got in the car again. Everyone was in a cheerful mood. That's what happens when you make someone else genuinely happy.

"I know a charity that accepts children's toys and clothes. That will be our last stop." Richard said.

"Wait, I know a better place." Annabel leaned forward and whispered something in his ear.

"Are you sure?"

"Yes, trust me."

The children shared glances with each other.

"So where are we going?" George asked, hoping to get an answer.

"You'll see." Annabel replied.

Shortly after, they pulled up at an orphanage.

"Is this the place?" Maggie asked and looked out the window.

"Yes, now get the boxes and ring the door bell." Richard said as they all got out.

"Why the orphanage?" He asked Annabel when all the kids got the boxes and headed up the stairs to the orphanage door.

"Because, I don't think the younger ones quite understand how happy and excited people get when you give them something nice. Earlier, we gave the boxes to the organizations, they were happy, yes, but the reaction of the person actually receiving whatever it is inside the box is ten times better. Especially that of childrens. So, they'll really see the impact of their kindness and hopefully, this encourages them to be kinder." She said.

"That's very thoughtful of you." He put a hand around her shoulders and pulled her in to his side, placing a kiss on her head. How could she be so perfect? He found himself thinking. He fell in love even more.

They walked up to the orphanage when the door opened up and the kids were beckoned in. They got in to see excited kids, from different ages, open up the boxes and pull out the toys and clothes.

There was excited chatter, laughter, and playing. Even the Pelton kids got involved in all the fun. They all got invited over to stay for dinner and because the orphaned children were so happy and excited for them, they couldn't say no. Richard even offered for all the children to come up to their house every once in a while to change things up. They could enjoy the fields, the stream, taking care of the horses, and activities in the house.

"Sorry, I didn't get your opinion on inviting them over." He said to Annabel when they were helping with picking up the dishes.

"Why would you need my opinion though?"

"It's just that- I thought- never mind." Richard has gotten so used to having her around, being a mother to his children, and them literally acting like a married couple that he totally forgot that they weren't married and in a relationship, so he technically didn't need to get her opinion, especially since she's just an employee. But that thought didn't sit right with him. He didn't have to technically ask her, or seek her opinion, but he wanted to. It made him feel better, and if he got her approval, it made him feel like he was doing a great job. And he didn't like thinking that she was just an employee. She was much much more than that. She's the women he loves and wants to spend the rest of his life with. She's the women he wouldn't mind getting down on one knee for right this instance. Her opinion did matter, it always did.

"Why would I not want to get your opinion? It's my house just as much as it is yours." He recovered from his little stumble of words.

Annabel looked up at him and flicked soap at his face. She was washing and he was drying the plates and cutlery.

"Sure." She sarcastically said.

"It is." He insisted and wiped the soap off. "Don't you want it to be?" He dared to ask.

"Well-I mean-what?"

"Nothing."

A Family Trip to Town and Ice Cream Fun

"Wait no, go back!" Maggie said as they were driving down to town.

Annabel went back to the previous station and watched as Maggie's eyes lit up.

"Your daughter has excellent taste in music." She grinned and glanced at Richard driving beside her, who gave her a side eye and a smile.

It was spring break and Richard told everyone that they could spend the entire day in town doing whatever they wanted.

"Monroe is my favourite!" Maggie exclaimed.

"Would you like to go to the movies and see if they have anything of hers playing?" Richard asked and Maggie squealed in happiness.

"Margot and I will have to go shopping for new shoes. She grew out of all her current ones." Annabel said as they all began to climb out of the car when they arrived at the movies. She knew Margot wouldn't be patient enough to sit still for the entire movie, so it was best to not waist time and get things done. "Would anyone like me to get them anything, or we'll all go shopping together after you watch the movies?"

The twins and Maggie said they'll go after and George had plans to meet up with Tiffany afterwards, so he won't be with them.

"Oh, umm, yeah. Can you get me new socks?" Richard absentmindedly said.

"Yeah, you did say you ripped holes in nearly all of yours a few days ago." Annabel said, rummaging through her purse.

"They're totally acting like they're married." Maggie said to George and he snickered, agreeing with her.

"Yeah and I also need new undergarments. Mind getting those for me darling, or if it's too embarrassing-"

"No no, I got it. Don't worry about it." She said, finally pulling out her handkerchief and handing it to Margot to wipe her nose.

"Oh, alright. Thank you. You take care."

"Sure, you too. Enjoy the movie."

"Of course."

Then, they both turned to each other, kissed and went on their merry way.

The kids stood flabbergasted.

"Did you..."

"Just see that?"

George and Maggie finished each other's sentences.

"Oh my word." Sam gasped.

"Since, uh, when?" Tam said.

"Holy crap, and it looked so natural too." Maggie grasped George's arms.

"So, they've kissed before..."

"And clearly, many many times."

The twins and the older siblings ran to catch up with their father who was already in the building.

"Oh, I was wondering were you loot disappeared to." He said.

"Papa! You just kissed mama!" Maggie said.

"Oh really? I didn't even realize." He said without a care to the world. "Pick out a movie now will you?"

"S-sure."

*

"I'm tired." Margot whined.

"Hi tired, I'm mama." Annabel grinned and Margot giggled.

"That's not my name!" She laughed.

"Then why did you say it was?" Annabel laughed with her.

"Because I'm feeling tired." Margot explained as she skipped beside Annabel down the sidewalk.

"I see, well, isn't that Papa just up ahead? We can tell him that we're ready for lunch." Annabel said, and when Margot paused, confirmed it was actually her father and ran to him, Annabel waved her hand in greeting and Richard spotted them.

"I thought you'd get more stuff." Richard said when he meet up with Annabel.

"I have all I need, so I didn't need to go shopping for myself. I just got the kids the pieces of clothings they needed."

"I thought we said we'd go shopping together, after the movie." Maggie said, feeling slightly sad.

"We did, and you are. You'd be bored if you went shopping for stuff you needed, so I did that myself. You can go shopping for stuff you want, there's a difference." Annabel's lips tilted upwards at the happiness in the kids eyes.

"Can I get some toys? I need some." Sam asked.

"Are toys a need or a want?" Annabel asked, and they all began walking down the side walk together, headed to the toys store.

"What do you mean?" Sam asked, not really getting the difference.

"A need is something you need in order to survive. Water, air, food, shelter, and clothes. Some people have a few more needs than others, and a want is something that you can live without. Extra toys, books, clothes, cars, basically things that make your life more enjoyable. Things you want." Richard said.

"Oh, well then I want a toy." Sam said, understanding what the difference was.

"How'd I explain it?" Richard asked, whispering to Annabel. They were both walking behind their children to keep a better eye on them.

"Couldn't have said it better my self." She reassured him and they side fist bumped each other.

"Have I told you already? But you look rather ravishing darling." He grinned and placed a hand in her back pocket of her shorts.

"Richard!" She gasped in slight surprise but kept her voice down. Her cheeks burned up, but she didn't make a move to remove his hand from her behind.

"Lunch after toys?" Margot asked and slowed down so she was walking in between them and Richard reached down to hold on to his daughters outstretched hand, taking his hand off of Annabel.

"Sure sweetheart." He warmly smiled at her, but he still had a cheeky look on his face.

Annabel lightly tapped his bum, which got him to squeeze them in surprise, and she walked up ahead to join in on Maggie and Tams conversation like she did nothing.

He got all tingly on the inside and extremely happy that she was being silly with him. Everyday she gives him a new reason to fall in love with her all over again.

*

"I'm stuffed!" Tam groaned and fell back in her chair.

"George's missing out." Sam said.

"He's with his girlfriend." Maggie said girlfriend in a funny way that got both the twins to snigger and laugh.

"When are you getting a boyfriend Maggie?" Margot asked and Annabel immediately put her hands on Richards lap and put her weight into them, effectively stopping him from jumping up and causing a scene.

"We will not be talking about boyfriends in front of your father. And what makes you think that if Maggie got a boyfriend we'd tell papa?" She said and Richards head snapped to her and his jaw dropped in shock.

"Annabel! You wouldn't tell me!?" He gasped and looked very hurt.

"Not if you're going to cause a scene, I'm not." She said and took her hands from off his lap. "I'll find a way to slowly bring it up to you though."

"As long as you tell me. I can't believe you have such little faith in me. What makes you think I'll cause a scene?"

"You were just about to jump up and overreact over an imaginary scenario." She said and went back to eating her food. "If that's not causing a scene, than I don't know what is."

"I think that's a reasonable reaction." He grumbled.

"It's not." Both Maggie and Annabel said.

*

"Do you guys mind if you wait here for a bit? I just saw one of my friends and I'd like to go greet him." Richard motioned up a head on the sidewalk and they all said sure.

"Say, mama, can we go get ice cream from that store over there?" Maggie asked. It was a store just up ahead, where Richard was standing talking to his friend.

"I don't know, see what your papa thinks."

They ran up to their father to ask.

"What did mama say?" He asked, stopping mid sentence with his friend to pay attention to them.

"To ask you."

"Oh, alright then. Let me just-" he began pulling out his wallet but the kids already ran back to Annabel to tell her.

"Okay, then here you go, but make sure you come back quickly. I'll wait here." She handed them five dollars each and they excitedly ran into the shop.

Richard saw the exchange and his heart warmed up. His friend looked between him and Annabel and then it clicked.

"Ahh, I see. She's Annabel."

Richard snapped to him.

"How do you know her?"

"I don't. I heard about her. Everyone was curious who the mysterious woman was that Richard Pelton danced with, leaving his fiancée so quickly for her. She was gorgeous in that dress, let me te- alright, okay, I got it. I'm not going to talk about her like that. She's your girl." He stopped what he was saying when he saw the murderous look on Richards face.

After a few minutes of waiting, Annabel noticed a few men leaning on a building behind her, checking her out, which was making her feel extremely uncomfortable. She really wished for the them to just leave and now, she regretted wearing shorts out. She started to fidget when she heard the comments they were saying and her palms began to sweat. And she just wanted to disappear when she heard their footsteps approaching her.

"Hey sexy, why are you just standing around like that?"

She ignored them and didn't turn to face them.

"Hey! My friends talking to you." One of them harshly gripped her shoulder and spun her around.

"Leave me alone." She pulled her shoulder away.

"You're so beautiful though." The first guy said and looked her up and down like she was an object.

When she didn't respond he got angry and spat by her feet.

"Fuck you! I said you look beautiful be greatfu-"

Then out of nowhere a fist came flying and crashed into the man's face, blood spilling out of his nose.

"Fucking ass hole." Richard growled out loud and pounded the man to the ground while his friend took on the guy that touched her. "Don't go anywhere near my woman you hear me?" Richard got up when the man looked nearly dead and spat on his face and drove his heel into his stomach, for good measure.

The guy was on the ground, beated to a pulp with blood everywhere. Richard looked at the remaining guy with bloodlust in his eyes, but not wanting the same fate as his two bleeding friends, he was wise and ran away. Leaving the two of them behind.

Richards friend got up from beating the man he was with and kicked his rib cage.

"That's the guy that touched her, right?" Richard said and came forward to him. He crouched down so he was face to face with him. "Maybe I should just cut your hands off? Wouldn't that be nice? The army will cover up for me anyways and no one will care."

Richard pulled out a switch blade from his pocket and held it up so the nearly unconscious, bloody man could see it. That switch blade was always with him, after fighting in World War Two and having the constant anxiety of being attacked without a single weapon on him, that switch blade brought him peace of mind when it was in his pocket.

"No! Please! I'm sorry! I'm sorry! We didn't know she was taken!" The filthy man cried and tried to scramble away, but Richard pressed the knife to his throat and he froze as tears ran down his face.

"It doesn't matter. You touched my woman. You shouldn't have." He put pressure on the knife and a trickle of blood flowed down the man's neck. Annabel squeezed her fists at the scene in front of her. It's nothing she hasn't seen before, in fact, this was a lot less gory then seeing injured soldiers on hospital beds with gashes and bullet wounds. She was just slightly surprised at how malicious Richard was being, she's never imagined seeing him in a scene like this, so she doesn't know how to react.

Richards friend saw her clench her fist and interpreted it as her not being able to handle all the blood being spilled. He stepped in front of Annabel, holding one of his arms back and the other forward in protection.

"Richard, that's enough. I don't need you accidentally killing him." He put a hand on Richard's shoulder and pulled him away. Richard actually wanted to keep going, but he was afraid all this blood will make Annabel uncomfortable.

"Leave. And take that asshole with you. If I ever see you near her again I will not hesitate to kill you." Richard said with so much menace that the man looked about ready to piss himself. Richard put the knife away and watched as he pathetically tried getting up,dragging his friend with him.

Richard quickly turned around and pulled Annabel in a bone crushing hug and squeezed his eyes shut as he felt tears welling up. He was slightly bent over so his chin was resting on her shoulder. He breathed as much of her as his lungs could allow.

His friend immediately left the two of them alone and went into the ice cream store to make sure the kids don't come out and interrupt them.

"I'm so sorry. I'm so, so sorry. I didn't come on time and he touched you with his filthy hand and made you feel uncomfortable. I'm so sorry that I'm not good enough a-and I couldn't keep you safe. You mean the entire world to me. You make me happy and feel like I'm safe and I couldn't do that with you. A-and..." he squeezed her tighter, "I love you so much, I can't- I can't."

He was about to start hyperventilating with the constant thought of what those three men could have done to her, adding on the fear of rejection from her since he confessed.

And when she squeezed him back and turned her head so her face was resting, facing the side of his neck, he knew it was all okay.

"You couldn't have come at a more perfect time. Thank you for keeping me safe and out of harms way. It makes me feel good to know I have someone like you that has my back. Someone that makes me feel extremely happy and loved. I couldn't have asked for anyone better, you're perfect Richard. A-and I've wanted to say it for a while too, but I've been scared."

"What is it." He said, finally pulling away so he was studying her face. She tentatively reached up and brushed some of his tears away. "You don't have to be scared with me."

"I know, I just, was. But I'm not anymore."

He leaned his cheek into the palm of her hand.

"Than what is it?"

"I just wanted to say, I love you too."

The shock on his face was as clear as day.

"Y-you love me?"

"Yes, I thought I was pretty obvious with it, seeing that Tiffany continually teases me about it."

"Tiffany." He grumbled, still not liking the fact that George got a girlfriend without telling him.

"She's a nice girl you know?"

"Oh I have no doubt," he sighed and they pulled out of the hug and held each other's hands as they walked to the ice cream store.

"Then why do you get so upset?"

"Because George thinks he couldn't have told me. He thought I wouldn't approve or something, or maybe that I wasn't worth telling?"

"I'm sure that's not the case."

"It definitely is."

"You're only going to make yourself feel even worse if you keep talking like that."

"I'm a depressed man, what can I say?"

They laughed but got all serious really quickly.

"I shouldn't make fun of a mental illness like that."

"No, you really shouldn't. But at least you're aware."

"Mhm. But just to make sure, you really love me? Even with my limp?"

"I love all of you."

*

"Did we make you wait too long?" Richard said as they walked into the ice cream parlor and to the kids table.

"Why are your hands all bloody like Uncle Eric?" Maggie said, deciding to ignore that his fingers were laced with Annabel's.

"Love makes men crazy." Eric told her and patted her head.

"That doesn't explain your bloody fists."

"Brothers in arm always stick together." Was his explanation. If Annabel really was the women that Richard, his best friend, his brother, has fallen head over heels for, then that makes her his sister. He couldn't let those guys have their way with his sister.

"So you got in a fight?" Sam asked excitedly.

"I beat them up! You should ha- no, no, what are you talking about? Fighting is bad. Yes, very, very bad. Unlessyou'reprotectingMamathengoallout." He said the last part quickly because Annabel was death glaring him, but he still got slapped upside the head.

"Go wash your fists, both of you." Now she was glaring at Eric who gulped in nervousness. Although she just met Eric and wasn't even properly introduced to him, she got brotherly vibes from him.

"Let's go mate, or we'll both die today." He grabbed Richards collar and dragged him to the bathroom.

"Did he really get in a fight?" Maggie whispered to her and she subtly nodded. "That's so cool!"

*

"Mar mar, your ice cream is melting." Annabel pointed out while taking a spoonful of her own sundae.

"Oh."

But it didn't matter, it already dripped down her shirt and skirt.

"What did you get?" Richard asked as he came back with his banana split ice cream.

"A sundae, and I just, like, added a bunch of sprinkles." Annabel replied.

"It looks fun and delicious. Can I try some?"

"Sure."

She gave him a spoonful and his eyes lit up.

"It's really good. I feel bad ordering what I have now." He pouted, not that he did order it.

Annabel pushed her ice cream across the table towards him and took his.

"Have mine. By the way, since when do you like bananas? I thought you hated them."

"I do. It's just Eric was being an as-amazing friend and thought it would be a great idea to order me the banana while I wasn't paying attention, he's still waiting for his." He failed to mention that he was too busy smiling silly at watching her laugh at something one of the children told her.

"A great friend indeed." She sniggered and as if Eric heard what they said, all the way from where he's standing at the counter, he turned around and smiled wide, and when the kids weren't watching, he gave them the finger.

Memories &The Engagement

T hey all arrived back home beaten up and exhausted from a fun day in town. Margot even began crying at the last bit of the evening because of how tired her feet were, but luckily, she slept throughout the entire car ride back.

"I'll help you with the kids." Richard groggily mumbled.

"Mm, thanks." Annabel said, picking up Tam who was giving her grabby hands. Richard picked up Margot from the back seat and George tugged on a stumbling Sam.

"Come on almost there, lad." George heavily sighed and then decided to pick him up to save time.

"Night." Maggie groaned and pulled herself up the stairs and into her room.

"Sweet dreams Gigi." Annabel called out and they trudged into the younger kids room. "Thanks for helping George."

"Sure, night." He placed a kiss on her head and dragged his limbs to his room.

"Sleep tight." Annabel replied.

"Where do I sleep?" Eric stumbled into the room.

"I'm still wondering what you're doing here." Annabel groaned.

Eric hadn't gotten in the car with them, but still managed to arrive at their house ten minutes before them. They found him sleeping on the doorstep.

"Even I don't know. I just found myself here." He mumbled and laid down on the carpet, immediately falling asleep.

"Should we get him a bed?" Richard peered at his friend and nudged him with his foot, but he didn't move.

"No, leave him to suffer back pain in the morning." Annabel tugged at Eric's hair but he still didn't budge. "Dead as a horse."

"I feel dead." Richard groaned as he put Maggie in her bed without changing her, they didn't want to wake her up so they just took her socks and shoes off.

"Same."

Annabel changed a half sleeping Tam that barely had enough energy to keep standing and was heavily leaning on her.

Richard was trying to change Sam who made the floor his bed, next to Eric.

"You're finished?" He asked when he was done and was standing at the doorway waiting for Annabel so he could shut the door.

"Just a moment." Annabel kissed the kids heads, was kind enough to get Eric a blanket and then walked out the door and to her room.

"Are you...?" She began to ask but just let it drop.

"Yeah." He said and followed her into her room.

"Do you have...?" He began to ask but let his voice trail off. Both of their eye lids were nearly shut.

"Yeah, in that drawer."

"Thanks." He pulled out a pajama set from the drawer with an new underwear and went to change in the bathroom while she changed in the room.

They both finished changing at the same time, Annabel turned the lights off and they both flopped onto the bed on their respective sides. Their heads missing the pillows by a few centimeters, but they didn't feel like moving.

"My feet, they feel like bricks." Richard groaned his face was half mushed into the comforter.

"And mine like cement blocks." Hers too was half mushed into the comforter.

"Isn't that just bricks?"

"Are bricks made out of cement?"

"I don't know, do you?"

"Would I have asked you if I knew?"

"Fair enough. Hey, so like, when did you fall in love with me?"

"Hmm, I don't know. I've always liked you. And my feelings continued to grow, I only recognized it as love a little over a while ago. How about you?" She asked.

"Mm, I think that time you got the kids covered in whip cream. I started falling in love there."

"That's a long time ago."

"That is, now that I think about it."

"You, you have the capacity to think?"

He lightly shoved her and she broke out in giggles which caused him to smile and turn his entire face into the comforter, because her giggling got butterflies in his stomach.

They lapsed into a moment of silence before Richard broke it.

"So I've been thinking-"

Annabel gasped.

"He can think!" And then she burst out in giggles again. "I'm sorry! I'll stop I promise. It's just when I get really tired I act like a drunk for some reason." Then she burst out into giggles again and rolled around until she was on top of Richard. Her back over his, and they just laid there.

"So what have you been thinking?" She said and held in another burst of giggles.

"Do you want to get married?"

She blinked.

"Sure, but not now. How about when summer break starts, before George leaves for university."

He blinked.

Just like that? She agreed that easily? He expected her to brush him off. They did just say their I love you's today. Why would she agree?

"Why did you agree?"

"Didn't you get the answer you wanted?" She rolled off him so she was laying beside him.

"I mean yes, I just didn't expect you to actually agree."

"Don't be silly. We've both loved each other for a while now, and we already act like we're married. It's no brainer I'll agree, really. Or did you want me to say no?"

"No! I wanted you to say yes, I just-"

"Then there, you don't need to think about it any longer. I love you, and I wouldn't mind getting married right now, but it's not very ideal to do it now."

Richard brought an arm around her and pulled her to his chest. He curled up in a ball around her body and breathed her in.

"I love you Annabel."

"I love you too Richard."

"Just so we're clear, we're engaged now right?" He mumbled into her hair.

"I guess so."

"Oh my word, I can't believe we're getting married." He said and then burst out in a fit of laughter.

"I know right. Us? Getting married? Who would have thought?"

She turned her head to look at him and then they both burst out in another fit of giggles.